"So, it's not really a marriage you're proposing, it's a straight-out trade. Your money for my name," Morganna said.

"That's the deal," Sloan replied.

"Usually, you know, it's older guys who have divorced their first wives who are looking for a trophy to display."

"I was too busy fifteen years ago to find someone unsuitable to marry, just so I could discard her now in order to acquire you. You don't appear to have any time to lose, Miss Ashworth. Are you interested or not?"

Morganna raised her chin and looked him straight in the eye. "Convince me that what you're offering is worth the price you're asking."

To have and to hold...

Their marriage was meant to last—
and they have the gold rings to prove it!

To love and to cherish...

But what happens when their promise
to love, honor and cherish is put to the test?

From this day forward...

Emotions run high as husbands and wives discover
how precious—and fragile—their wedding vows are....
Will true love keep them together—forever?

Marriages meant to last!

Look out in December for
Part-Time Marriage (#3680)
by Jessica Steele

HIS TROPHY WIFE
Leigh Michaels

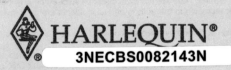

HARLEQUIN®

3NECBS0082143N

TORONTO • NEW YORK • LONDON
AMSTERDAM • PARIS • SYDNEY • HAMBURG
STOCKHOLM • ATHENS • TOKYO • MILAN • MADRID
PRAGUE • WARSAW • BUDAPEST • AUCKLAND

For Dan Thompson
of the Kansas State Fire Marshal's Office.
Thanks for the wholehearted way
you threw yourself into this project!

ISBN 0-373-03672-8

HIS TROPHY WIFE

First North American Publication 2001.

Copyright © 2001 by Leigh Michaels.

Visit us at www.eHarlequin.com

Printed in U.S.A.

PROLOGUE

His office was seriously out of style these days, compared to the sleek corner suites occupied by many corporate executives. It didn't boast deep carpeting or antique furniture or original art. And its windows didn't show off a stunning panorama of a landscape or a city skyline or even a sunset. Instead Sloan Montgomery's very old-fashioned office lay almost at the center of the building that housed Sticks & Stones, and its windows overlooked the production line. That arrangement had been the standard in industrial design eighty years before, when the building was new, and Sloan had never seen any reason to change it. He could keep a closer eye on the furniture being built down on the factory floor when all he had to do was turn around from his desk to take a look. And he had always been able to think better with the rumble and whine of the machines in the background.

His right-hand man, the controller of Sticks & Stones, tapped on the half-open door of Sloan's office. "Here's that information you wanted." He laid a folder on the corner of the desk. "The credit report is right on top. It's not a pretty sight."

Sloan's fingers itched to reach for the folder, but he schooled himself to patience. This had waited a long time; it would last a minute longer, till he was alone. "Thanks, Joel."

The controller showed no inclination to leave. Instead he moved around the end of the desk to stand with his back to the stream of warm air coming from the space heater which warmed the office on cold mornings. "I know it's none of my business—"

Very true, Sloan thought.

"But I can't get straight in my mind why you want all that information. As far as I can see, Burke Ashworth had nothing to do with Sticks & Stones. He wasn't a competitor or a supplier. He wasn't even a customer, and thank heaven for that, because it appears he owed money to everybody but us in three states by the time he drove his car off that bridge."

"There are more ways to be in debt than by owing money, Joel."

"I suppose you're right." Joel sounded doubtful. "It appears that he did it on purpose. Drove off the bridge, I mean. There was still a suicide clause on his life insurance policy."

"So he was trying to make his death appear to be an accident?"

Joel nodded. "Not very successfully, I'd say. Look at the whole picture. He was up to his neck in debt with no way to pay it off. About the only thing he actually owned was the car he was driving, and it's just scrap metal now."

"He could have declared bankruptcy."

"From what I've heard, Burke Ashworth would rather be tragically dead than look like a loser. Besides, filing for bankruptcy wouldn't have done him much good—the federal government doesn't forgive things like unpaid income tax. No, a convenient accident was his only way out. I couldn't locate a single asset that hasn't already been spoken for by a half-dozen creditors."

Now there, Sloan thought, his controller—good as he was—had missed the mark. For Burke Ashworth *had* left behind an unencumbered asset. Just one.

He had left a daughter.

And if Sloan played his cards right, Morganna Ashworth would pay off her father's debt. Every last fragment of it.

CHAPTER ONE

Six Months Later

THE four of them were laughing over some silly thing—
Morganna didn't even remember what it had been—when
she caught a glimpse of the dainty platinum watch on her
wrist. "Time for me to go home," she said, pushing her
chair back from the bridge table. "Sloan will be back
from San Francisco today."

"And the little wife wants to be waiting to welcome
him home from his business trip," said the redhead sitting next to her. "Even after half a year of marriage—
how touching."

From the seat on Morganna's other side, a brunette
rolled her eyes. "Don't be sarcastic, Sherrie. You know
perfectly well if it was you instead of Morganna that
Sloan was coming home to, you'd be standing by the
front door waiting for him."

"For Sloan Montgomery? Not on your life," Sherrie
said. "I'd already be in the bedroom."

They all laughed, but Morganna had to make an effort.
And she noticed as she looked across the table at her
hostess that Emily's amusement, too, was only on the
surface; her eyes were not smiling.

"It really isn't fair, Morganna," Sherrie went on.
"He's not only gorgeous, but all you have to do is murmur that you want something, and you've got it. Your
house, that rock on your left hand, your new car—talk

about the woman who has everything. Even if the rest of us were lucky enough to stumble onto a guy who'd buy us anything we wanted, trust me—he'd be eighty-two and toothless. Sloan is everything a woman could want.''

The envy which dripped from Sherrie's voice seemed to turn to sulfuric acid against Morganna's skin. But, she told herself, it was crazy to resent Sherrie's perceptions of her marriage, when the woman had picked up precisely the image that Morganna had worked very hard to project.

Emily walked her to the door. ''Sherrie and Carol mean well, Morganna. They just don't know what they're talking about.''

''And that's exactly the way I want to keep it.'' Morganna forced a smile.

It wasn't even that the two were so far off track, she admitted to herself as she turned her new sports car toward the gated neighborhood of Pemberton Place and the Georgian-style mansion she called home. Sloan *was* gorgeous—and he was generous to a fault. Morganna had quickly learned to be careful of what she admired, for whatever she looked approvingly at was apt to turn up on her breakfast tray within a day or two. After a few episodes, she'd learned to bite her tongue.

She'd slipped up on the car, though. She'd commented—without even thinking about it—that the new convertibles looked like fun. Less than a week later, hers had shown up in the driveway. It was even her favorite color.

Sherrie was right—Sloan was everything a woman could want. So why was Morganna so unhappy?

She parked the convertible in the garage next to Sloan's black Jaguar. The presence of his car didn't mean he was home, however; it had been sitting there all week while he was gone. She'd offered to take him to the airport and to pick him up on his return, but he'd said he didn't want to put her to the trouble and he'd called a cab instead.

Of course, she thought with a hint of bitterness, a trophy wife wasn't supposed to be practical, only decorative. And that was all she was to Sloan Montgomery, Morganna knew—a trophy. A mile marker of how far he had raised himself. He'd gone from the factory floor to the owner's office, from a walk-up apartment to a mansion in Lakemont's most exclusive neighborhood, from the wrong side of the tracks to an alliance with one of the oldest and best-known families in the city.

She knew quite well what she was to him—because he'd told her, on the day he had proposed marriage, precisely what he wanted her to be. A symbol, visible to all the world, of his success. A trophy wife.

She let herself in the side door and in the shadowed corridor she almost bumped into the butler. He'd been hovering, she thought—waiting for her. Wanting to warn her, obviously—but of what?

"Is Mr. Montgomery home?" she asked.

Selby's voice was lower than usual. "Not yet, Miss Morganna. I believe his plane should be landing any time."

"Then what's wrong? And don't tell me that nothing is, because I can see by your expression that you're worried."

Selby's tone dropped even further. "Your mother is here. None of us knew she was coming, Miss Morganna. She just appeared on the doorstep this afternoon."

And that, Morganna knew, signaled trouble. Obviously Abigail Ashworth hadn't come all the way from Phoenix to Lakemont, Wisconsin, for afternoon tea, or simply for the fun of the trip. More to the point, she didn't make a habit of dropping in uninvited. In fact, this was the first time since she'd moved to Phoenix, right after Morganna's wedding, that she'd been back. Though Morganna had made it plain that her mother would always be welcome in her house, Abigail Ashworth had pointed out that the Georgian mansion was now Sloan's home, too, and she couldn't take his hospitality for granted.

Yet now she had done exactly that. *Big trouble,* Morganna thought grimly. "Where is she?"

"In the miniature room."

Morganna started across the hall to where a nine-foot-tall pocket door stood open a couple of inches. She pushed the walnut panel back and stepped inside.

Despite its name, the room itself was anything but miniature. In fact, it was one of the largest in the house, intended by the builders to be a music room with plenty of space for dancing. Its contents were what had given the room its name, for it was full of tiny treasures. Some of the diminutive dolls and accompanying furnishings had belonged to Morganna's grandmother, but most had been gifts to Morganna herself, souvenirs from her travels, or items she had created on her own. Half-museum, half-workshop, the room was Morganna's favorite in the entire house.

Literally at the center of the collection, standing on a specially built cabinet in the middle of the room, was a miniature reproduction of the full-size mansion. Architecturally correct down to the most infinitesimal detail, it was more museum piece than plaything, even though it had been Morganna's birthday gift the year she was nine.

She looked past the dollhouse to her mother. Abigail

Ashworth sent a vague smile in her daughter's direction and straightened the fingernail-size envelopes in the brass mailbox beside the front door of the miniature house.

"I'm sorry I wasn't here to greet you," Morganna said.

"Why should you be waiting for me, dear, when I didn't let you know I was coming?"

At least that answered one question, Morganna thought. Her mother wasn't confused about whether she'd been invited. Not that she'd harbored any real doubts about Abigail's mental faculties. "It's a nice surprise to see you, of course. But I have to ask, Mom—what brings you back to Lakemont at this time of year?"

"You know Indian summer was always my favorite season."

"Believe me, that's going to be over any day. The evenings are already getting so damp and chilly that a fire feels good."

Abigail sighed. "All right. If you must know, there's a man."

Morganna's jaw dropped. Her mother, in love? "Here?"

"No, in Phoenix. He's moved into the apartment complex, and he seems to think he's in love with me. The more I try to discourage him, the more determined he gets."

That made more sense. "So you're escaping from him?"

"I feel sure that if I'm simply unavailable, Robert will find someone else to focus on. Heaven knows Phoenix has no shortage of eligible women." Abigail smiled brightly. "A month or so should do it, I think."

A month. Morganna's heart sank, but she forced a cheerful note into her voice. "That's great, Mom. It seems we never have enough time together anymore to do everything we'd like, but with a whole month... Has Selby given you a room?''

"Yes, dear. And I'm going upstairs to it right now, so you and Sloan can have your reunion without an audience.'' Abigail winked and turned toward the door.

Morganna forced herself to wait long enough for her mother to reach the top of the stairs before she ducked back into the hallway. Sloan was due to walk in at any moment, and she had to intercept him. She simply could not take the chance that he'd run into Abigail without warning. Surprised, he might slip up—and if he said one wrong word...

Morganna was standing by the front door and calculating times in her head—if his flight was on schedule, if he'd had no trouble getting a cab, if rush hour traffic had been no worse than usual—when she saw an airport limousine maneuver through the gates of Pemberton Place and pull up in front of the mansion. By the time Sloan got out, she had the front door open and was hovering just inside.

Sloan paused on the sidewalk. The light of the decorative lamps at the front of the house fell in sharp angles across his face, highlighting the rugged good looks which always took Morganna's breath away for an instant whenever she first laid eyes on him. The effect was stronger than usual today—but then it had been nearly a week since he'd left. He wasn't wearing a coat, only a dark-gray wool suit, and at thirty-five he was as lean and athletic-looking as most men who were a decade younger.

Without haste, Sloan shifted the weight of his garment bag and briefcase and climbed the shallow steps to the entrance. "This is a surprise,'' he said dryly. "Finding you waiting by the door for me. But you've forgotten the good little housewife's standard props, haven't you? Pipe, slippers, newspaper, martini—''

Irritated, Morganna said, ''You don't smoke, it's too early for slippers, you've no doubt already read the newspaper and you don't like martinis. And there's a very good reason why I'm standing here.''

''There must be. I never doubted it.'' Sloan set his bags down and looked her over, his dark eyes intent. ''And you're not very happy about the reason, are you? Well, let's go somewhere private and you can tell me about it.'' He reached out as if to drape an arm around her shoulders.

Morganna had already moved toward the drawing room. Once inside, she sat on the edge of a chair and said, ''My mother's here. And she's planning to stay a while.''

''That's nice.''

''*Nice?* Are you out of your mind?''

''I like Abigail. Always have.''

Then it's too bad you didn't marry her instead of me, Morganna wanted to say. She bit her tongue hard. ''Well, I like her too, Sloan—too much to let her be worried, or to suspect that we're not happy.''

Sloan moved over to the drinks tray, poured himself a whisky and handed Morganna a club soda. ''In other words, you don't want her to know the price you paid so she could have her comfortable life in Phoenix.''

''What good would it do if she found out?''

''None, of course. You can rest easy, Morganna—she won't discover it from me. Of course, it may be more of a challenge for *you* to pretend to be deliriously happy.'' He picked up his glass and left the room. From the hall, she heard the deep murmur of his voice, and then the butler's softer reply.

Morganna rubbed her temples. The irony in his voice was like an ice pick to her heart. Where had she gone so wrong?

It had all seemed so logical, so straightforward, when it had begun—just over six months ago, and barely a week after the world had caved in on Morganna and her mother.

It had been several days after Burke Ashworth's fatal car accident before Morganna had begun to realize the perilous situation her father had left them in. But as soon as she started to absorb the facts, confirmation crept in from every side. The banker calling to demand payment on the mortgage, the stockbroker announcing with regret that the value in Burke's portfolio was not adequate to cover his margin calls—those things were only the beginning of a downhill slide that seemed to have no bottom.

That was probably why, when Sloan Montgomery had shown up at the house, Morganna had agreed to see him—even though she barely knew him. Because, she thought, talking to him couldn't possibly make things worse.

The memories of that day were carved into the very cells of her brain. She'd been sitting with her mother in the drawing room, receiving callers. A horrifying percentage of them had turned out to be her father's creditors, and though she had tried to convince her mother that there was no need to see each and every one, Abigail insisted. Morganna could only watch with helpless anxiety as Abigail's exhaustion reached crushing proportions. It wasn't until the stream of creditors had ended that Abigail finally agreed to go and rest.

Just then Selby had brought in a business card, neatly centered on a silver tray. Morganna could have screamed at him.

Abigail took the card, her hands trembling with fatigue. "This must be another one, because I don't recognize the name."

Morganna looked over her shoulder. "No, Mom. This one's for me."

Abigail checked the card again and looked suspiciously at her daughter. "You know this Sloan Montgomery? Then why haven't I heard of him?"

"Because there's never been any reason to mention him. Remember the fund-raiser for the women's shelter that I helped with last year? I met him then. He builds furniture in a factory down in the old commercial district on the lakefront—innovative, unusual stuff that he designs himself—and he donated a bunch of it to the shelter. That's all I know about him." She looked up at Selby. "Show Mr. Montgomery into the miniature room, please. Tell him I'll be with him in a moment, and close the door. Once he's out of the way, Mother can slip past without being seen and go up to her room."

Abigail had wearily agreed, and a few minutes later Morganna had let herself quietly into the miniature room.

Across the room, Sloan Montgomery was standing by Morganna's worktable, apparently studying a lyre-backed dining chair, smaller than his palm, that she'd been carving on the day her father died. "My furniture is a little different from yours, I'm sure," she said, and he straightened and turned to face her.

Against the background of tiny things, he looked even larger than life—impossibly tall and broad-shouldered in a dark gray pin-striped suit. He was every bit as handsome as he'd been at the fund-raiser, but today he was somber—more so, surely, than a condolence call on a casual acquaintance would require. The tension in his face made Morganna pause. She was worn-out herself, or perhaps she would have thought twice before she asked, "Which category are you in?"

He frowned. "I beg your pardon?"

"I find myself wondering why you're here. I assumed this was a sympathy call—but perhaps it's just another attempt to collect an unpaid bill instead. Did my father owe you money, too?"

"No, he didn't. And though I'm sorry about your loss, this isn't really a sympathy call, either, Miss Ashworth."

Morganna frowned. "Then—if you're not intending to console me or regain what you're owed, why have you come?"

"To try to take your mind off things."

"Now that's refreshing," she said lightly. "And a great deal different from the rest of our visitors today. Half of them seemed to remember my father as a saint, while the rest were obviously biting their tongues to keep from saying what they thought of him. And those were just our friends—the creditors didn't bother to mince words. After all that, I could stand a little entertainment. Do you sing? Dance? Play the accordion?"

"I gather that you and your mother are in troubled circumstances."

"If that's what you call taking my mind off things—"

"Perhaps I should have said instead that I came to find out whether I can help you."

"I don't see how," Morganna said frankly. "*Troubled circumstances* is putting it lightly. Daddy's been dead just a week, and it's quite apparent that life as we have known it is over."

He nodded. "The house?"

"It's as good as gone—it was in his name, and it's mortgaged for more than it can possibly sell for. I suppose we could fight the bank and at least get a delay in the foreclosure, but to be honest, we can't even afford the utilities. Mother's already terminated the staff—though bless their hearts, they're staying on a few days despite being laid off, because they don't want to leave us here alone."

"There's no money at all?"

If she hadn't been so exhausted, so tired of going over it all in the squirrel-cage of her mind, Morganna might have been offended at the question. But it didn't occur to her to bristle at the personal nature of the inquiry. Perhaps from the outside the problem would look less thorny, more malleable—and she and Abigail needed all the insight they could collect.

"Nothing significant, compared to what he owed." She sighed. "Even if the insurance company pays off—and I can't blame them for not being eager to settle up—it won't be enough. I don't know what we'll do. Mother always left all the financial details to Daddy, but unfortunately ignorance is no defense. Just because she didn't know his deals doesn't mean she isn't going to be held responsible for at least some of them. She's going to end up worse than penniless. And she's got no skills to support herself, much less to pay back debt—she's always been a stay-at-home wife. Besides, she's just close enough to retirement age to make finding a job very difficult, but too far away from it to get any benefits."

"But your father's debt comes to rest with her, right? It's not your problem."

Morganna bristled. "She's my mother. Of course it's my problem."

After a little pause, he asked, "So how are you planning to pay it all?"

"Well, that's another difficulty," she admitted. "It wasn't very practical of me to get a degree in art. It's hardly a field that's in great demand these days."

"You could teach."

Morganna shook her head. "Even if I had the temperament, I don't have the right education to get a teaching certificate—it would take another two years of classes at least before I could qualify. And then we're back to the problem of money, because I could probably earn enough to live on while I went to school, but not enough to cover tuition, too."

"What are you going to do?"

"I start on Monday at the Tyler-Royale store downtown. A friend of mine is married to the store manager, and Jack—the manager—says I can arrange displays and try my hand at designing the storefront windows."

"That's a full-time job?"

"No, the rest of the time I'll be selling women's sportswear. It's a start."

She knew that despite her best efforts, she sounded tired and depressed. In a department store sales job, it would be decades before she could make a dent in her father's debts.

He said slowly, "I may have a better idea."

"I'm listening." Morganna shrugged. "Though I have to admit I not only don't see how you can help, I don't understand why you should want to, either. If you knew my father at all—"

It was apparent that he heard the question in her voice. "As a matter of fact, I never met him."

And then, while she was still trying to fathom why he seemed to feel responsible for her welfare and Abigail's,

Sloan Montgomery had looked her in the eye and asked her to marry him.

Morganna didn't remember fainting. The next thing she knew, she was sitting on the floor, her shoulders cradled in Sloan's arms, her nose resting against the soft lapel of his suit jacket, breathing in the delicious aromas of wool and soap and aftershave. The moment she was aware, however, she began to struggle, trying to get to her feet.

"Just sit there for a bit," he said. "The last thing you need to do is fall down again." He supported her till she could sit up by herself, and then he perched on her work stool, looking down at her. "Apparently my suggestion came as a shock."

"That's putting it mildly." Morganna wriggled around to brace herself against the cabinet which supported the miniature house. "Whatever makes you think I'd be interested in marrying you?" She saw his jaw tighten and added hastily, "I didn't mean that the way it sounded. It's just that we hardly know each other. The idea of getting married—"

"I think we know enough. I know, for instance, that the Ashworth name opens every door in Lakemont society."

"Not for much longer," Morganna said wryly.

"That's true." His voice was cool. "Unless you act quickly to limit the damage from your father's peccadilloes, a hundred years' worth of family history will go down the drain and you'll be an outcast."

"Do you think I care about that? My real friends—"

He didn't raise his voice, but his words cut easily across her protest. "And so will your mother."

Morganna bit her lip. It wasn't that her mother was

shallow, she wanted to say. But it would be even harder for Abigail to start over than it would be for her daughter.

Morganna had already noticed how many people who should have come to offer their sympathies had stayed away instead. She didn't think that fact had occurred to Abigail yet, but she knew that when it did, the realization would be devastating. Even the poverty they faced would be easier for Abigail to deal with than the humiliation of losing the only way of life she'd ever known.

—"Do you think I haven't tried to figure out a way?" she said wearily. "I can't simply conjure up enough money to bail us out."

"But I can."

She stared up at him. "Why would you want to?"

He looked across the room, over her head, and said calmly, "I don't suppose you'll find this flattering."

He'd been dead right on that count, of course—for what he'd told her then hadn't been complimentary in the least. He'd made it plain that it was not Morganna he was attracted to, but her social standing. With an Ashworth at his side, he'd be at the highest rank of Lakemont's society, and he would have achieved the final detail of the goal he'd set for himself as an impoverished kid years before—his own business, a few million in the bank, a position of respect in the community, a wife other men would envy him. Morganna was the ultimate piece in the puzzle he'd set himself to complete.

"So," she'd said, when the orange glow of her fury had finally dissipated enough that she could trust herself to speak without screaming at him, "it's not really a marriage you're proposing, it's a straight-out trade. Your money for my name."

"That's the deal."

"Usually, you know, it's older guys who have divorced their first wives who are looking for a trophy to display.''

"Sorry to violate the rules, but I was too busy fifteen years ago to find someone unsuitable to marry, just so I could discard her now in order to acquire you. You don't appear to have any time to lose, Miss Ashworth. Are you interested or not?''

Morganna raised her chin and looked him straight in the eye. "Let me make this perfectly clear. For myself, I wouldn't consider this proposition for an instant. It's an insult and I'd live in a cardboard box and eat cat food for the rest of my life before I'd make a deal like that.''

"But you have your mother to consider.''

"Exactly. So convince me that what you're offering her is worth the price you're asking.''

Sloan had convinced her. And he'd kept his word. The day Morganna married him, he'd taken over the responsibility for Burke Ashworth's debts, down to the last penny. And at the wedding breakfast, he'd handed Abigail a cashier's check—he'd told her it was the face value of her husband's life insurance policy—which would be adequate to keep her in comfort for the rest of her days.

Remember that moment, Morganna told herself. No sacrifice was too great a price to pay for the relief that had gleamed in her mother's eyes at that instant.

And no sacrifice was too great to preserve Abigail's peace of mind, even if it meant that Morganna had to spend every instant of the four weeks playing the part of a loving wife. Heaven knew she had perfected that role with her friends during the last six months—but performing for her mother would be a whole lot trickier.

It might be a challenge, Sloan had said, for her to

pretend to be deliriously happy. Well, he'd hit that one on the nose.

Deliriously happy. By the time the month was over, Morganna thought morosely, she'd be lucky if she wasn't simply delirious.

CHAPTER TWO

SLOAN dropped an ice cube into a glass and added a generous splash of liquor. "Here you go, Joel. Scotch on the rock—singular—just the way you like it." As he strolled toward the fireplace to hand over the drink, a log burned in two with a crack, and a shower of sparks surged up the chimney and flared against the fire screen. "Dinner will be in just a few minutes, but in the meantime you can bring me up to speed on what's been going on at Sticks & Stones while I've been away."

The controller didn't seem to hear. Though he took the glass, Joel continued to stare at the portrait in oils that hung above the drawing-room mantel. Following his gaze, Sloan contemplated the modernistic portrayal of Morganna—a much younger Morganna, hardly out of her teens—wearing a formal white satin gown, topped with a wine-colored velvet robe and an elaborate, glittery crown, which seemed much too heavy for her slender frame.

Reel in your tongue, Joel, he wanted to say. "That was painted the year she was Queen of the Carousel Ball."

Joel seemed to pull himself back from a distance. "Is that the big dance where all the year's debutantes are introduced?"

"And paraded around like merchandise," Sloan agreed.

"It's a beautiful picture."

Sloan looked at the portrait again. He found it fascinating that Joel liked it. Sloan had never been fond of the painting, himself, but he hadn't ever taken the time to figure out why. Was it the artist's style that turned him off? Generally he liked his art a little more realistic-looking. Or was it the too-fancy costume, which in his opinion made Morganna look like a child playing dress-up in her mother's clothes? Or was it perhaps the fact that the painting was from a time before he'd met her, a time when Morganna's world had been so far separated from his that there was no point of intersection?

Not that it mattered, of course; the painting was ancient history now. He hardly even noticed it anymore, except when someone like Joel commented. He turned his back to the portrait and leaned against the mantel, enjoying the warmth of the fire. "How have things been going at the factory while I've been away?"

Joel sipped his drink and settled into a chair beside the fire. "Well, there are several matters you need to know about. I got my hands on an advance copy of Furnishing Unlimited's next catalog."

Sloan's eyebrows raised. It was difficult even to get hold of a solid rumor about a head-to-head competitor's new products, but to have full information even a few days in advance of the formal announcements, set out in the competitor's own literature, was truly a coup. "How did you manage to pull off that one?"

Joel reached into his briefcase, propped against the chair leg, and handed over a slick magazine-size booklet. His voice was prim. "I really can't talk about my source."

Which no doubt meant, Sloan thought, that some woman on Furnishing Unlimited's payroll had slipped it to him. Obviously it wouldn't do to underestimate Joel; apparently a guy could be a ladies' man even with a calculator clipped to his belt and a pocket protector full of pens and pencils. "I wouldn't dream of asking for the details," he said dryly.

"They've developed a couple of new lines I thought you should see. I marked the pages for you."

Sloan flipped open the booklet, pausing at places where Joel had placed a sticky note, to look at Furnishing Unlimited's new line of modernistic office furniture. "This looks a bit like our current designs."

"That's what I thought. They haven't exactly done anything shady in adapting what Sticks & Stones did last year. But I believed you should know what they were up to, before it actually hits the market."

"I doubt they'll be able to lure our customers away with poor imitations of our designs, but you're right about the value of a warning. Put yourself in for a raise, Joel."

"Thank you, sir. I'll do that."

Sloan continued to flip pages. "You said there were several things to bring to my attention."

"We had to suspend a couple of workers this week. It seems they were running a business on the side, while they were on our time clock. The union steward was quite unhappy with the suspension action and is protesting it. And the men themselves, of course, were livid at being caught."

In the hallway outside the drawing room, a flutter of blue silk caught Sloan's eye. "I'll call all of them in tomorrow morning and get it settled," he said absently.

A moment later Abigail Ashworth appeared in the doorway. "Sloan, my dear," she exclaimed. "I'm so glad to have a moment with you before Morganna comes down. I feel I should apologize for my bad timing, though, popping in on your first night at home." Joel rose from his seat, and Abigail's eyes narrowed. "I beg your pardon, I thought you were alone."

"You remember my controller, Joel Evans?" Sloan said, and she nodded. "A glass of wine, Abigail?"

"That would be lovely, dear. You know, it's awfully good to be home—I could almost thank Robert for making my life so stressful that I couldn't wait to get out of Phoenix. I'm sure Morganna has told you my silly reason for being here." She looked expectantly up at him.

He was just opening his mouth to answer when, from the doorway, Morganna said hastily, "Actually, I haven't had time, Mother."

Sloan's momentary irritation at her interruption—didn't she think he could handle her mother?—gave way to a wicked impulsiveness. "First things first," he murmured. "I'm sure you understand, Abigail, that there are certain...priorities...when a newly married couple is reunited after a time apart."

He watched in fascination as Morganna's face went pink. He was reasonably sure that the cause of her heightened color was pure fury at him for the suggestive comment, but it was equally apparent to Sloan that the onlookers had interpreted it differently. There was a naughty but appreciative gleam in Abigail's eyes, while Joel shifted his feet and looked thoroughly embarrassed.

Sloan reached inside his jacket and pulled out a long, slender, black velvet box. "That reminds me, darling. Since I had other things on my mind earlier, I forgot to give you the anniversary gift I brought you from San Francisco."

Morganna shook her head. "It's not our anniversary."

"Yes, it is. It'll be six months next week since our wedding." He held out a hand in summons, and watched her closely as she slowly crossed the room toward him.

Though he was certain Joel and Abigail saw only a pretty hesitancy at claiming her gift, Sloan couldn't miss the bone-deep reluctance with which she moved. She'd have been more eager, he thought, to approach the guillotine.

Her dark green dress was one he'd seen her wear at least a dozen times before, and he idly wondered which point she was trying to make tonight by wearing it instead of something new. Was she emphasizing her reluctance to shop for clothes because spending his money left her feeling even more in his debt? Or was she subtly pointing out that she didn't think he was worth dressing up for?

In public, where her friends or his business associates might notice, she was always a fashion plate, elegantly garbed and groomed and seldom wearing the same dress twice. If he'd remembered to tell her earlier that Joel was coming for dinner, Morganna would no doubt have come downstairs looking as if she was off to the Carousel Ball immediately after dessert. Sloan had suspected on occasion that she was actually trying to look like a caricature of the leader of society he'd said he wanted her to be.

In private, however, things were different. Though to a casual onlooker she would always have appeared just as neat and well-turned-out, she was in fact far less elegant. She wore the same few dresses—all ones she had owned before their wedding—and she ignored the stock of jewelry with which he'd supplied her.

Probably, he thought, she would like him to believe that on the nights they dined alone she was in the habit of simply seizing the first thing she touched in her closet, without even noticing what it was. In fact, he thought it was more likely that she deliberately planned what she wore, and how often, in the hope of annoying him.

Not that her campaign of irritation would succeed. It didn't matter to Sloan if she wanted to wear the same dinner dress for the next thirty years—especially if it was this particular dress, which hugged her figure with its deceptively demure shape and enticed despite an innocently high-cut neckline. He suspected if Morganna had any idea precisely how attractive he found that dress, she'd have donated it to the thrift shop long ago.

"That old thing again?" he murmured as she came within arm's length. He took her hand and drew her closer, till his lips brushed across her cheek. "Your wardrobe is becoming incredibly boring, my dear."

She said under her breath, "I'll keep your objections in mind."

"Meaning that you intend to go right on wearing the same old clothes. Perhaps I should mention the problem to your mother."

"You wouldn't."

"Don't push me." He laid the velvet box across her palm and let a husky note creep into his voice. "Happy anniversary, darling."

He saw the flash of irritation in her eyes, but obediently Morganna unsnapped the box and lifted the lid. Inside, on a bed of black satin, lay a river of fire—a bracelet of diamonds too numerous to count, perfectly matched and set into a braided chain of platinum that had made him think of her pale blond hair.

Irritation had given way to dismay, he saw as she raised her gaze to meet his. Her eyes were stormy blue-gray, and one crystal tear clung to her dark lashes. "Stop this," she whispered. "Stop torturing me."

He bent closer. "It's a gift, Morganna."

"It's a ball and chain, and you know it."

He lifted the bracelet from the box. "Would you rather put it on or explain to your mother why you don't want to wear it?" He watched her swallow hard before she

held out her hand. He fastened the bracelet; then raised
her wrist so he could press his lips against the pulse point.
Deliberately he pitched his voice just above a murmur—
suggestively low, but just loud enough for the two onlookers to hear. "I'll wait to get my real thank-you later,
when we're alone. Now, I think Selby is making signals
about dinner. Shall we go in?"

The bracelet seemed to weigh a thousand pounds, and
every time Morganna raised her fork, the diamonds on
her wrist caught the light from the chandelier and shattered it into knife points that hurt her eyes.

Six months, she thought. It would be six months next
week since the wedding. Since the first and most osten-
tatious of the gifts.

She had been taken completely off guard at the wedding breakfast, when Sloan, after giving Abigail her
check, had handed Morganna an envelope containing the
deed to the Georgian-style mansion—a legal document
detailing that the property now belonged jointly to Sloan
Montgomery and Morganna Ashworth Montgomery.
Husband and wife.

"Just a little wedding gift," he'd said, and Abigail had
exclaimed in delight at the idea that her daughter's childhood home and the multitude of treasures it contained
were now Morganna's to keep.

Morganna herself had shuddered at the thought—not
because she didn't want the house, for she had shed tears
over the thought of losing it, but because the image of
debt piling upon debt made her stomach churn. Only then
did she realize that somewhere in the back of her mind
she had cherished the vague hope of being able one day
to pay back the money he had provided for her mother,

so she could be free of Sloan Montgomery. But how could she ever be free if she, too, took from his bounty?

Under her breath, without looking at Sloan, she'd said, "I didn't ask for anything from you. And I won't take anything from you."

Sloan had leaned across her to top off her already-full champagne glass. "That's your tough luck, Morganna, because I'll give you anything I damned well want to."

In startled silence, she had turned to stare at him.

"I understand quite well that you'd prefer being a martyr to accepting my gifts. Living in a cardboard box and eating cat food—wasn't that what you told me you'd sooner do than marry me?"

Morganna's voice was taut. "Don't expect me to believe you did this out of fondness for me. You only put my name on this deed to impress my mother. If you'd been doing it for me, you'd have made the house mine entirely."

"I could have wiped out your father's debts outright, too, instead of promising to pay them off over the next couple of years. But do you think I'm such a fool that I'd hand you everything you want at a swoop in return for nothing but a promise? We made a deal, Morganna. Now that you're my wife, you have an image to maintain, and part of your performance is to graciously accept the generous gifts of your seemingly smitten husband. Get used to it."

She'd had six months to become accustomed to Sloan's way of doing things, but it hadn't made a difference. Six years wouldn't change things, either, she thought wearily, if—God forbid—it came to that.

It wasn't that his gifts were garish or ill-chosen. Showy as the diamond bracelet was, it was in perfect taste; the quality of the stones was what made the bracelet so at-

tention-getting, not a flashy setting. It was the motivation
behind the gifts that Morganna found so hard to swallow,
and the fact that her wishes didn't enter into his plans at
all.

And why should she expect him to consult her, she
wondered bitterly. It would be silly to ask a department-
store dummy what she wanted to wear; a plastic man-
nequin had no opinion. And, it was all too clear to
Morganna, that was precisely how her husband viewed
her. She was nothing more than a prop in his magic
show—a bit of stage dressing to help convince the audience how stupendous her husband was.

So Morganna did what she had to do. In public she
was the perfect trophy, smiling and happy, wearing diamonds Sloan had chosen and designer clothes purchased
with his money. In private, she wore what she liked. And
if he was tired of seeing her hunter-green dinner dress,
that was just his tough luck, because she intended to wear
it till it was threadbare. Fortunately it was one of her
favorites; if she'd hated the dress she might not have been
as eager to annoy him with it.

After dinner the men excused themselves to finish their
business discussion, while Morganna and Abigail returned to the drawing room to sit beside a freshly stoked
fire. Morganna hardly noticed the passage of time or the
drift of the conversation until her mother said, "I expected by now you would have redecorated the drawing
room, Morganna."

"I think it's fine the way it is, Mother." *And to re-
decorate would simply add one more item to the list of
things I owe Sloan.*

"Don't be silly, child," Abigail said flatly. "I know
for a fact that you've always disliked the dark hangings
that I put in here. And I have to admit, at this time of

year and with winter closing in, it's a gloomy sort of
room—not at all the cozy feeling I was trying to achieve.
Perhaps the depressing atmosphere in here is why you
seem to be drooping tonight.''

Morganna seized the excuse. *Tomorrow,* she thought,
I'll be able to handle this. But not tonight. ''I was hoping
it didn't show—but I am tired, Mother. If you don't
mind, I think I'll go on up to bed.''

''I don't mind at all, dear. I'll just walk up with you
and get my book.''

At the foot of the stairs, Abigail paused. ''Aren't you
going to say good-night to your husband?''

The very question startled Morganna, and she had to
stop and think about how a normal married couple would
act. That reaction alone showed how shatteringly peculiar
their situation was, she thought. ''I'm sure he'd rather
not be disturbed, Mother. When he's talking business
with Joel—''

''Nonsense,'' Abigail announced, and before
Morganna could protest she'd knocked at the library door
and pushed it open.

Sloan paused in the middle of a sentence and looked
inquiringly at them. ''Sorry to interrupt,'' Morganna said,
more abruptly than she'd intended. ''I just wanted to say
good night.''

She was already backing out of the doorway when
Sloan moved toward her. ''Is it so late? I'm terribly sorry,
darling.'' He looked over his shoulder. ''We're almost
finished, aren't we, Joel?''

The controller shook his head. ''I'm afraid not. There's
still the matter of updating all the property insurance on
the factory, and there's also a customer problem that
came up while you were gone.''

Sloan shrugged. ''Then it will be a little longer,

Morganna. In case you're asleep by the time I come upstairs—'' He slipped one arm around her shoulders, and
with the other hand he cupped her chin and raised her
face to his.

Morganna had opened her mouth to object before she
thought better of it, so her lips were parted when he
kissed her. She tensed at the first brush of his mouth,
panic rising in her. Even at their wedding, he hadn't
touched her this intimately, and every cell in her body
shrieked in protest.

As her reluctance surged, Sloan's arms tightened,
drawing her even closer. Though she knew his embrace
must have looked like that of an experienced and wel-
comed lover, Morganna couldn't mistake the steel that
held her fast. She couldn't have broken free from his hold
even if his kiss, soft as the graze of a butterfly's wing,
hadn't turned her knees the consistency of oatmeal.

She was trembling by the time he let her go, and he
steadied her for a moment with both hands on her shoulders. "Unquestionably," he said huskily, "I've been
gone from home much too long."

By the time he finally got Joel out the door, the house
was quiet. Even the butler had taken Sloan's advice and
gone on to bed. Yawning, Sloan scattered the embers in
the library fireplace, put the last of his papers in his briefcase and checked the locks before he climbed the stairs.

In the upper hall, he paused for a moment to listen to
the silence and looked thoughtfully down the hall to the
closed door of Morganna's bedroom. Though that good-
night kiss had been intended as pure theater, it had not
remained a simple performance for long. But he hadn't
had enough time to fully assess Morganna's reaction to
the embrace. At first she had been annoyed, certainly,

and reluctant—those feelings had exuded from every
muscle as he'd held her. But there had been something
else as well, something he hadn't quite been able to iden-
tify before he'd had to let her go. It wasn't anger that
had made her go weak in the knees. Had it been the faint
flutter of desire?—or had he merely seen what he wanted
to see?

As he opened the door of the master bedroom, instinct
made him pause for a split second to assess his surround-
ings. Was something actually wrong, or was the room
merely different? An instant later, he realized what had
prompted his caution, and his body tightened.

"Morganna," he said gently. Only then did he look
around, searching for an extra shadow in the darkened
room and spotting her in the window seat with her feet
drawn up and her arms wrapped around her knees.
"What gives me the singular honor of finding you waiting for me in my bedroom?"

She sounded almost petulant. "How did you know I
was here?"

Sloan touched one of the bedside lamps and it glowed
softly. "Your perfume. Midnight Passion isn't something
I'm used to smelling—at least not in this room. Next time
you try to hide, you might want to wash it off first."

"I'm not hiding. I need to talk to you."

"I was afraid it would be something like that." He
tugged his tie loose and dropped his cuff links in a tray
on the dresser. Without hurry, he began to unbutton his
shirt.

"Would you stop that?"

"What? Undressing? It's my room, I've had a long
day, and I'm tired. What do you want, anyway?"

"I want you to stop this preposterous behavior in front
of my mother."

"You told me you didn't want Abigail to have reason to suspect that we might not be quite as happily married as she'd like."

"Yes, I did." Her admission was obviously reluctant. "But you don't have to pretend that we can't keep our hands off each other. Your attempt at demonstrating affection was rude and distasteful."

"To whom? It seemed to me that toward the end you were starting to enjoy it."

"Don't be ridiculous. Besides, you were contradicting yourself."

He frowned. "How exactly am I supposed to have contradicted myself?"

"First you made it sound as if we rushed right off to bed the instant you got home. Then when I came in to say good night, you implied that we hadn't done anything of the sort."

"And how did I do that?"

"*I've been gone from home much too long,*" she quoted, sounding impatient.

"Oh, that." He grinned. "Your mother probably thought I meant it was time to rush off to bed again. After a whole week's absence, you know, once would hardly be—"

She had turned faintly pink. "Well, you've made your point, Sloan. You can knock it off now." She stood up. "Oh—and don't get any crazy ideas about why I'm in your bedroom, now or any other time."

He draped his shirt over the back of a chair. "Are there going to be other times?"

"Probably." Morganna sighed. "Mother came upstairs with me tonight."

Sloan was honestly puzzled by the switch of subjects.

"What's that got to do with anything? Where else could she go? The guest rooms are all on this floor."

"She lived in this house for thirty years, Sloan—she knows where the master bedroom is. I could hardly stroll down the hall to my room with her standing outside the guest room door watching me. So I came in here instead."

He shrugged out of his shirt and kicked off his shoes. "I see. If we were a normal married couple, we'd be sharing this room—and that's what she expects. I get it."

"Good for you. Unfortunately it's likely to happen again. I just want you to understand that any time I have to spend in your bedroom has nothing to do with you."

"So what are you planning to do with all the time you'll be waiting? I suppose we could sit on my bed and play penny-ante poker every night until you're sure Abigail's asleep and you can sneak down the hall to your own room. But how are you planning to keep her from noticing that when Selby brings up your breakfast tray in the morning he doesn't deliver it to the master bedroom?"

It was obvious from the way she caught her breath that Morganna hadn't yet considered that difficulty.

"And considering your fondness of breakfast in bed," Sloan mused, "I doubt you'd find it appealing to get up at the crack of dawn every day so you could beat her downstairs."

"I suppose we could knock a hole in the wall between your closet and mine so the suites connect." Her voice dripped sarcasm. "That way I could just stroll through your bedroom every time I want to go to my own, and you wouldn't have to put up with my presence for any length of time."

"Not a bad idea, but I think she'd ask questions about

the noise and the workmen. Anyway, my suggestion is much less dusty than yours.'' Sloan walked into the bathroom and reached for a toothbrush. ''Move in here with me,'' he said over his shoulder.

''Pretend to share a bed? That would take more acting than I want to think about. I suppose we could take turns sleeping on the window seat, but she could be here for the next month.''

''I didn't say anything about pretending.'' Sloan smeared toothpaste on his brush and started to count off the seconds, betting with himself about exactly how long it would take her to react.

Before he'd reached five, Morganna was standing in the bathroom door. ''If you think for a single moment that I'm actually going to sleep with you, Sloan Montgomery—''

''Not a single moment,'' he conceded. ''I've been thinking it for more like six months.''

He brushed his teeth for a full three minutes, dividing his attention between watching the silently shifting expressions on her face and cataloging the contents of the bathroom. It was fortunate, he decided, that he didn't own a straight-edged razor, because if she couldn't get her hands on one, she couldn't slit his throat with it—no matter how much she looked as if she'd like to try.

''No.'' The single word sounded as if she were strangling.

He pretended not to have heard. ''I've been meaning to talk to you about this anyway. You've had six months to get used to the idea of being married, and now it's time to take the next step.''

''This has never been a marriage, it's a merger.''

''Up till now, yes. But really, Morganna—you're

surely not naive enough to think I intended it to stay that way.''

"But you already have everything you wanted from me! The house, the listing in the social register, the trophy wife on your arm at parties—for heaven's sake, Sloan, they're going to ask you to be one of the official hosts at the Carousel Ball!''

He was momentarily distracted. "I must admit I'd like to know how you pulled that one off, Morganna. But what makes you think that's all I wanted?''

"What else is there?''

He said, slowly and very deliberately, "I want the Montgomery name to have the same respect in future generations that the Ashworths have had in the past. In short, I want my children to be accepted as the cream of Lakemont society.''

Her eyes were wide and unfocused, as if she was looking at a scene too awful to comprehend. "Your children—and mine, you mean? No.''

"Why? Because you think your bloodline is too rarefied to mix with a barbarian's?''

The dart struck home; he saw her shudder. "Because you're not interested in me that way.''

"Of course I am. I'm no monk, and you're a very attractive woman.''

"But in six months you've never even suggested... You only kissed me tonight because Mother was watching.''

"I've been biding my time, waiting for the right moment to take the next step. Tonight just made me think about what I've been missing and decide that the time is now. As for the idea that I'm not interested in you—I'll be happy to demonstrate how very wrong you are about that. Come here.''

She backed up instead. "Please, Sloan—don't be insulting. We both know I'm hardly the only woman who would have satisfied your requirements for a wife. I'm only here because at the moment you started shopping, I was available and my price was lower than most."

"Oh, I wouldn't say that. Do you have any idea what your father has cost me already? And I'm not nearly done clearing up the mess he left behind."

Her eyes widened. "If you think you can blackmail me into your bed by threatening to stop paying the debts you took over—"

"Coerce you by going back on the terms of our deal? Of course not. I wouldn't do that any more than I'd use force."

He saw relief register in her face.

"I've been very patient, Morganna. You've had six months to get used to the situation. I've given you every opportunity to see the advantages of being married to me, and I've made it plain that I intend this to be a long-term bargain. It's time to move on to the next stage of the relationship. Make it a real marriage."

"I suppose you set this up." She sounded bitter. "Inviting my mother, I mean, so she'd put pressure on me."

"Not guilty. As a matter of fact, Abigail's visit startled me just as much as it did you. I'll admit if I'd thought of the scheme, I might have engineered it—"

"That's certainly no surprise."

"But I didn't think of it. Her timing is very convenient for my purposes, but then it's no crime to take advantage of handy accidents. Do you know, I think I've looked at that dress quite long enough for one evening. Shall I help you out of it, my dear?"

She folded her arms across her chest. "You said you wouldn't use force."

"And I won't—because I don't need to. You'll come to me, Morganna."

"I'm leaving now." Her voice was shaky.

He didn't move to intercept her as she made her way across the room, but he didn't step out of her path, either. "You'll come to me," he repeated softly, "because if you don't—"

She stopped less than two feet away and turned to face him. "Because if I don't—then what? You'll tell my mother on me? How ludicrous can you get, Sloan?"

Sloan shook his head. "Because if you don't, you'll regret it. Not because of anything I'll do, but because of what you'll be missing, Morganna." With a single step he closed the distance between them and cupped her cheeks in his hands. Her breath was shallow and uneven; he could feel her panic in the rigidity of her face. "Whether you know it or not, you have appetites, my dear. And I intend to be the man who satisfies them."

CHAPTER THREE

WHERE his fingertips had rested, Morganna's skin burned as if he had branded her. And by simply cupping her face in his hands, he'd apparently done something to her balance, too, for she stumbled over thin air as she fled down the hall to the quiet safety of her own bedroom.

Her mind was spinning. She'd known from the beginning that Sloan drove a hard bargain, but she had assumed that he would stand by his word. She hadn't realized till tonight that the man was a snake—keeping his real agenda hidden until it was too late for her to back out of their deal.

I want my children to be accepted...

She shuddered at the very idea. How she had managed to keep her voice steady enough even to answer him was beyond her comprehension.

My children, he had said. Not *our children.* That had stung. Not that she'd have found the more inclusive description any more inviting, of course. No matter what the circumstances, she was hardly likely to grow starry-eyed over the notion that Sloan wanted her to carry his child. Even if he'd pretended romantic interest in her, she wouldn't have been swayed.

In fact, however, the phrase was simple confirmation of what Morganna had known all along—that to Sloan she was nothing more than a means to an end. Any of a half-dozen other women she could think of would have been just as acceptable to him as Morganna was—as his

42

wife, his ticket into Lakemont society, the mother of his children....

Children. The nerve of the man!

But he had made one mistake, Morganna told herself. In his almighty confidence, believing that all he had to do was crook his finger and she would fall into his arms like an overripe fruit, Sloan had sworn off the one approach that might have actually gotten him what he wanted. He had disdained the entire idea of using force. And he had scorned the use of coercion—which in Morganna's opinion was just about the same thing.

You'll come to me, he had said, without either pressure or duress being brought to bear. But in that, he was dead wrong. Morganna could not imagine any circumstances which would make the idea of a real marriage palatable to her. The notion that she would cheerfully volunteer for wifely duties was farcical.

It was long past time for Sloan Montgomery to be taken down a notch. Now Morganna just had to figure out exactly how to do it.

Morganna had finally gone to sleep, repeating over and over her determination to wake early enough to be downstairs before her mother rose. It shouldn't be difficult, she told herself, no matter what Sloan thought. Her mother was no more a morning person than Morganna herself was. Besides, Phoenix was two time zones later than Lakemont, and Abigail's internal clock would take a few days to adjust. She might even sleep till noon.

But Morganna's rest had been fitful, and somewhere in the middle of the night her subconscious decided to ignore the orders she'd given. As a result, the household was wide-awake by the time Morganna roused. The first thing she heard, in fact, was Sloan's voice just outside her bedroom door, and the novelty of it made her abruptly sit upright, her heart pounding. He never came to her room. For him to be there this morning, after the incredible demands he'd made last night—

"I'll take that tray, Selby," Sloan said. "Good morning, Abigail. I'm sure Morganna will want you to come in, but let me check first to be sure she's at least got a nightgown on by now. Earlier this morning…well, you know…"

Morganna's hand curled on the first object she could reach, which happened to be the bedside phone—but she knew throwing it at him would only add to her problems. As the door opened, she forced her fingers to relax.

Sloan, already dressed for the day in black trousers and a herringbone jacket, backed into the room with her breakfast tray in his hands and kicked the door shut behind him. He stood for a moment just inside the room, surveying her.

Morganna was painfully aware that the neckline of her teal satin pajamas plunged even lower than that of the average ball gown, and she knew it was apparent that she was wearing nothing except the thin, clingy satin. But she was equally determined not to admit that she'd even noticed his inspection, much less that it had raised her hackles. So she smothered the urge to draw the blankets up to her shoulders. "You haven't learned to knock? Or were you hoping to catch me before I had a chance to make myself decent?"

"I thought your mother would expect me to have the run of the place." He set the tray on the side of the bed and sat down beside it. "And as for looking decent— you're a lot more than decent. In fact, you're downright tasty this morning."

"How sweet of you to notice. However, let's not

change the subject away from my mother." Morganna's voice was low but full of acid. "I'm so glad we had that heart-to-heart talk last night, Sloan, so you'd know exactly how to go about sabotaging my efforts. You understood perfectly well that I didn't want her to know about this room, so of course at the first opportunity you made sure to point it out to her!"

"She was already in the hall. So was Selby, on his way to deliver your breakfast. At that point, keeping Abigail from finding out that we don't share a room was no longer an option, Sleeping Beauty. The question now is damage control. So what would you rather she think? That your private and personal bedroom is really an armed fort complete with moat, or that we've made an amicable arrangement to use two rooms in order to preserve our mutual comfort?"

Morganna bit her lip and thought it over. "I guess, when you put it that way..."

"I thought you'd see the sense of it." He pulled the door open again. "Come on in, Abigail. I'll ask Selby to bring an extra cup."

"I don't want to interrupt," Abigail began.

"Please do," he said gently. "As a matter of fact, your daughter was just giving me a piece of her mind."

Morganna tried to smother her gasp.

Sloan didn't look at her. "She didn't want me to confess to you that I snore so badly that she moved out of our bedroom."

It wasn't bad for a spur-of-the-moment story, Morganna thought. It might even work.

Sloan leaned over the bed and gave a playful tug to her satin lapel. "It seems that my beloved doesn't want to admit to you that I might be less than perfect."

The back of his fingers brushed, not quite innocently,

against the slick satin over her breast. Automatically Morganna tried to pull away, but her restless sleep had left her too tangled in the sheets to move far.

"I can certainly understand that philosophy," Abigail agreed.

"Besides, she thinks it's much more romantic when I come dashing in from down the hall to help fasten her dress. Or, for that matter, to unfasten her dress..."

"That'll be enough," Morganna muttered.

Sloan grinned and bent closer. "Would you rather say thank you for the rescue now or later?" he murmured. "I could ask your mother to step outside for a few minutes. And there's nothing so pressing at the office that it can't wait for a little while."

"Later," Morganna said through gritted teeth. "*Much* later."

"Good. Anticipation makes everything better, I've found." He pushed a lock of her hair back and his lips brushed the sensitive skin just under her ear. Then he straightened. "I'll take you both out for dinner tonight."

As soon as he was gone, Morganna tossed a pillow toward the foot of the bed. "Make yourself at home, Mother. You're up awfully early, aren't you?"

Abigail hitched up her tailored trousers and settled onto the bed. "Not really. I've gotten in the habit of playing tennis at 6:00 a.m. It gets so hot in Phoenix in the summer, you know, that early morning is the only reasonable time to exercise. And with the time difference, this is just exactly when I'd be getting ready to hit the court. What are your plans for the day, darling?"

"I really don't have any," Morganna admitted.

"Well, you mustn't rearrange your schedule to suit me. I have friends I can call, you know, when you're going to be busy. Though we really must do some shopping sometime.''

"Sloan wasn't supposed to tell you—'' Morganna stopped abruptly.

"Tell me what? That you could use some clothes? Do you think I can't see that for myself? Honestly, dear, that dress you were wearing last night is at least three years old. You wore it when you were Emily Hamilton's bridesmaid.''

"I still like it.''

"Then let's look for something similar. In purple, maybe—that would look nice with your coloring. And don't tell me you don't have the money. Considering things like that diamond bracelet, I doubt Sloan keeps you on a short allowance.'' Abigail paused. "In any case, I've always felt badly that I didn't have time or money to do more in the way of a trousseau for you, Morganna. But now that I'm settled so well, I'd like to make up for that.''

With Sloan's money. Morganna bit her tongue and didn't say it. She couldn't voice her suspicions to Abigail that it might have been Sloan himself and not the life insurance company who had provided that sizable cashier's check to secure her mother's future. As long as Abigail had no reason to believe she was living on her son-in-law's charity, Morganna couldn't bear to hurt her by suggesting it. It wasn't as if she had firsthand knowledge, after all—only a bone-deep fear that even Sloan couldn't have forced the company to pay a claim they didn't feel they owed because the policyholder had so clearly committed suicide.

"Sure, Mom,'' she said with resignation. "I'd love to go shopping.''

"And while we're out,'' Abigail added briskly, "I

need to stop at the country club pro shop and get some tennis balls.''

"There should be some in the hall closet downstairs. And you can borrow my racquet, if you didn't bring yours.''

"Racquet? Oh, no, dear, I just need the balls. But they must be brand-new ones. And I'll have to buy some light-weight fabric, too. Is your grandmother's old sewing machine still set up in the back bedroom?''

Morganna was startled. "Yes. But whatever do you need it for?''

"To sew pockets in the back of Sloan's pajama jackets, just big enough to hold a tennis ball. It will keep him from sleeping on his back, and that's supposed to be a sure-fire cure for snoring.'' Abigail frowned. "Unless... Honey, he *does* wear pajamas—doesn't he?''

Sloan never walked into his factory without remembering the first day he'd stepped onto the property, as a high school student looking for a part-time job. In maintenance, if there was nothing else, he'd told the personnel officer who'd talked to him. He was fairly handy with a wrench, and there was no question he could operate a broom. He must have sounded as desperate as he felt, for with a sigh the personnel officer had sent him up to the office which overlooked the factory floor, to talk to the boss.

What old man Brigham had seen in the young man, he'd never told anyone—but he'd put Sloan to work that day. Within a couple of years, Sloan could operate every machine in the building. And on the day that Brigham announced that he was closing down the firm and retiring, Sloan had once more gone into the office overlooking the factory floor. This time he asked the boss to sell him the business instead of liquidating it.

"I don't know why you think you want it, son," Brigham had said. "Nobody's interested in buying this factory. Furniture's a hard trade to be in, and with labor costs so much cheaper outside this country, it's a fair bet that you'll be undercut on every side."

"I have some ideas," Sloan had said laconically, and, after surveying him for a long time, Brigham had agreed to give him the chance. Out of respect for the old man, Sloan had waited till after Edward Brigham's funeral to change Brigham Furniture's name to Sticks & Stones. The new name would have given the old man an instant ulcer, but it was a far better reflection of the reputation Sloan was building as the creator of innovative, sometimes even funky, bits of furniture for home and office.

It hadn't been an easy road, and Sticks & Stones still hit speed bumps from time to time. He'd encountered a good-size one just this week in San Francisco, as a matter of fact. But every time he walked into the factory and paused to sniff the scents of wood shavings and fabric dyes and machine oil, he reaffirmed that buying the business had been the right decision. Sticks & Stones had been good to him.

The day shift was already running at full speed when he arrived, and Sloan took his time crossing the factory floor, greeting workers, checking product quality, listening to the hum of the machines. By the time he reached his office, he was eager to throw open the windows overlooking the assembly line below, settle into his big leather chair and plunge into the mess that must have accumulated during his absence.

He was startled to find Joel sitting at his desk, a mass of papers spread on the blotter in front of him.

Sloan paused. "I thought I gave you a raise last night, not a promotion. Isn't your office still down on the main floor?"

The controller half smiled. "I was afraid I might miss you when you came in, so I brought some work up to do while I waited for you."

"In that case, you might want some extra light on the subject." Sloan leaned over the desk and flicked a finger against the metal finial atop the desk lamp. Instantly the bulb cast a pool of bright light over Joel's paperwork.

"No wonder I didn't see a switch," Joel grumbled. "I haven't run across a touch-controlled sensor in five years, since we quit making lamps."

"They have their problems," Sloan conceded. "But I like not having to fumble to turn it on. It's much easier to find the lamp in the dark than to grope for the switch."

Joel gathered up his papers and moved from Sloan's chair by the window to one on the opposite side of the big desk. "Why don't you throw out all this old stuff and use some of the furniture from our new lines? It would be a subliminal sales pitch to everyone who walks into this office."

"I like old things."

Joel's voice dripped irony. "I never would have guessed."

Sloan let his gaze drift around the room, from the scarred surface of Edward Brigham's teak desk, to the old wooden filing cabinets that lined one wall, to a row of child-size furnishings that occupied the space beneath the windows overlooking the assembly line. The small but perfectly scaled bureau and chair and sideboard were not toys, however, and they had never been intended to be used by children. They were the samples that salesmen of old had used to display their wares to prospective buyers. Nowadays, of course, it was no longer necessary to haul the real article around. But Sloan wondered sometimes if graphic designs and photos on a laptop computer were any big improvement. If he'd had the real thing with him in San Francisco, would it have made a difference?

"Besides," he said, "everything in here *is* our product—even if it's from an earlier era. So the subliminal sales pitch I'm making is that Sticks & Stones products last."

"It's awfully subtle," Joel warned. "I doubt most of our customers would get it."

"Besides, in this office, marble and glass and extruded aluminum would look out of place."

"And they wouldn't go particularly well with the aroma of antique dust, either."

Whatever Joel thought, the office was perfectly clean. But it did have a unique aroma composed of aged wood, furniture polish and the last remaining hint of old man Brigham's cigars.

Sloan leaned back, and the oak floorboard beneath the chair's wheel gave the same comfortable creak it always did. "So what's so important that you're waiting for me this morning?"

"I've arranged for those two workers we fired, and the union steward, to come in at ten."

"Fired? I thought you said you'd suspended them."

Joel shrugged. "It ends up being the same thing. Since they're not exactly repentant, I expect they'd start their business right up again as soon as they felt safe. And I've already talked to the insurance people this morning. They seemed to think the valuation you've put on the building is pretty high considering its age, but they agreed to go ahead and increase the limits on the policy, effective today, and send somebody out next week to confirm your estimates."

Sloan nodded. "They don't build factories like this anymore. There are beams in this building that are two feet square and span the whole width of the factory floor. Any value we'd put on that wouldn't be enough. Anything else?"

"I brought the file concerning that complaint I told you about. It's nonsense, of course, but the customer is pretty steamed and he insisted on talking to you. And I realized after I got home last night that we'd never talked about the outcome of your trip to San Francisco."

Sloan flipped through the folder Joel handed him. "They didn't say no."

"But they didn't say yes, either?" Joel gave a low whistle. "That's not good news."

"Not every sales pitch ends in an immediate sale, Joel." Sloan's voice was dry. "Surely you learned that much in business school."

"But that was a big one. I mean, supplying all the furniture to every branch nationwide of a major new chain of financial service offices... For them to ask you to come to San Francisco to make the pitch and then not say yes..."

"You think they might as well have said a definite no, because that's what they meant."

"Well..." Joel hesitated. "Yeah, that's exactly what I think. Now what do we do?"

"We look over the proposal again to be sure it's the best we can do, and then we let it ride and move on to the next possibility."

"I guess that gives me my marching orders for the day." Joel stacked his work and went out.

Sloan picked up a letter opener and tackled the stack

of mail on the corner of the desk. But the run-of-the-mill correspondence couldn't hold his attention.

Joel was right, of course. The lack of a definite answer, especially after a personal presentation, nearly always meant an ultimate refusal. And the San Francisco deal would have been the single largest order Sticks & Stones could hope for all year.

It was a good thing he was experienced enough in the business world not to have counted on that sale. Now that it appeared to have vanished into thin air, Sloan decided, he'd simply start to look for another.

Just as soon as he'd dealt with the suspended employees, soothed the feathers of the offended union representative and figured out how to please the unhappy customer who had surfaced while he'd been away.

As she often did when she felt particularly stressed, Morganna retreated to the miniature room in the late afternoon. Rhythmically kneading polymer clay till it was warm, smooth and workable always made her feel better. The next step, shaping the brightly colored bits into objects which could have been real if they only weren't so tiny, could almost always take her mind off her troubles.

She was so absorbed in creating precisely the right accessories for a boy child's bedroom that she didn't hear the pocket door slide open. Only the stirring of cool air that Sloan brought with him warned her that he was there.

Her fingers clenched, and the inch-high circus train that she'd been constructing turned into a misshapen lump. She put it aside and picked up another marble-size piece of clay.

Sloan leaned over her and picked up the discarded lump of red, yellow and blue clay. ''I see you're taking to modern sculpture now. Is the next project to be an art gallery?''

''No—that's what happens when you startle me.''

''But you told Selby to pass on the message that you wanted me. This makes two days in a row you've been waiting impatiently for me to get home. Better watch yourself, darling, this could get to be a habit.''

''Not likely. It's my mother again.''

Sloan pulled up the companion to her tall work stool and sat down. ''What's Abigail done this time?''

''Thanks to me, nothing.'' Succinctly she told him about Abigail and the tennis balls.

Sloan threw back his head and laughed heartily. ''So how did you dissuade her from this philanthropic project?''

''I told her that nothing would induce you to wear pajamas, so creating an antisnoring strait-jacket would be a waste of her time.''

He looked thoughtful. ''Is that the way you picture me, Morganna? Sleeping in the buff?''

''I wouldn't exactly call it a sexual fantasy,'' she snapped. ''The fact is, I could hardly let her rummage around in your room in search of pajamas, because who knows what she'd have found tucked in the corners of your closet?''

''Oh, I'm sure you'd have risen to the occasion. There's probably nothing more embarrassing than the odd pair of black lace panties, and you could always have claimed they were yours.''

Morganna rolled her eyes. ''But that's not the only problem. If she searched your wardrobe for pajamas and came up empty-handed, how could I have possibly have explained that you didn't own any after all, if I'd already told her you did?''

"You could have just turned slightly pink and murmured that though I'm not in the habit of actually wearing them when I'm with you, you thought I must surely own a pair or two. In any case, if you'd like to know for certain," Sloan said lazily, "you can stop by my room tonight and find out."

"I'd rather live with the suspense. You ungrateful wretch, you should be thanking me for saving you from her well-meaning interference. If she'd actually constructed this instrument of torture, you'd have had to report how well it worked."

"On second thought," Sloan said, "Maybe I should tell her to make a stab at it."

Morganna's jaw dropped. "Haven't you heard a single word I've said?"

"But you see, I couldn't possibly report how well it worked, because a snorer can't hear himself. Which means *you'd* be the one who'd have to report. And to do that—"

"I'd have to spend the night with you. If you think that feeble excuse is enough to get me into your bed—"

"Furthermore," Sloan said, "I'm betting that the next morning, if you were truthful, you'd have to tell her that I hadn't snored at all. Of course, I wouldn't have gotten a wink of sleep, either, if you were there—but that's beside the point, don't you think?"

Sloan took Morganna and her mother to a new restaurant, located in a renovated warehouse not far from the shore of Lake Michigan and only a few blocks from Sticks & Stones. Morganna had never been there before, and when Abigail wrinkled her nose at the idea of anything upscale locating in a warehouse district that had seen far better days, Morganna was inclined to agree.

"Wait and see," Sloan said. "I think you'll like the food—though I admit I have an underhanded motive for wanting the place to succeed."

"You're a part-owner?" Abigail asked.

"Not me. I don't know anything about the restaurant business. But it's handy for Sticks & Stones workers, and anything that keeps my people happy and gets them back to work on time is good for me. Besides, every upwardly mobile business that moves into the neighborhood makes my building more valuable."

Something about the statement nagged at Morganna. As soon as they were seated, she looked at Sloan over the top of her menu and asked bluntly, "Are you thinking of selling the factory?"

"What? No, of course not. Besides, there are still a whole lot of empty buildings down here—why would anyone pay the price for one that's occupied by a profitable business when they could buy an unused one for a fraction of the price? In the long run, though, if the neighborhood turns into a nightclub and boutique district—"

"The neighboring businesses might object to having a factory in their midst."

"They can object all they like, but as we were there first—"

The waiter approached, and Sloan broke off to look at the wine list.

Abigail glanced around the spacious dining room and admitted she was impressed. "At least there's room for the waiters to pass between the tables, which is more than you can say of most ritzy places."

"With the rent they have to pay in the pricey neighborhoods," Morganna said, "they have to cram in all the tables they can." She caught sight of a brunette standing near the maître d's stand and waved. "Look, there's Emily and Jack Hamilton. I wonder if they'd like to join us."

Sloan murmured something to the waiter. "Another advantage of the place is tables that are large enough to allow for a couple of extras."

Under cover of the greetings, Emily whispered, "You didn't say anything at bridge club yesterday about your mother coming."

"I would have, if I'd known. I'll tell you about it later."

"You look as if you could use a break. Want me to distract her?" Emily didn't wait for an answer; instead she hugged Abigail and was quickly absorbed in bringing the older woman up-to-date.

Morganna toyed with her wineglass and divided her attention between the two conversations at the table. Emily was right about one thing: it was restful just to sit and think of nothing. She already knew all the details of Emily's life, and it was only when she heard the word *fired* that she really tuned in on what Sloan was telling Jack.

"There wasn't much else to be done," Sloan said. "It turns out they weren't just running a private business out of my building, but the merchandise was only marginally legal. And they both had been in trouble before."

Morganna bit her lip. Of course, it made sense that he was telling Jack about his employee problems; as the district manager of the Tyler-Royale department store chain, Jack Hamilton dealt with troublesome workers every day, and if anyone could contribute a useful insight, it would be Jack. But deep inside her was a tiny kernel of sadness that Sloan hadn't confided in her instead of his friend.

Of course, Morganna reminded herself, she hadn't asked how his day had gone. But even if she had, he'd no doubt have passed the question off instead of answering, because they'd never gotten into the habit of sharing that kind of discussion....

Suddenly a matron in a huge, feather-decked hat loomed over the table, leaning across Morganna to shake a finger at Abigail. "So you're home," the matron said. "I knew Phoenix wasn't the climate to suit you for long. Of course, you've chosen exactly the wrong time of year to come back to Lakemont—unless you're home for the Carousel Ball?"

"I'm not certain how long I'll be here, Millicent," Abigail said.

"Well, you might want to stick around for that. Or, on the other hand, when you know the details, you might not." The matron frowned at Sloan, who had risen politely in greeting, and boomed, "As president of the Carousel Ball committee, I have been asked by my board to invite you to be a host at the ball next week."

Millicent Pendergast sounded, Morganna thought, as if she'd dutifully swallowed a very bitter pill, carrying out her duty but making it clear that she thought the decision an ill-advised one. It was apparent that Sloan had heard the same lack of enthusiasm in the matron's voice, and Morganna winced at the dangerous sparkle that sprang to life in his eyes. She tried to draw his attention, hoping to keep him from making matters worse, but Sloan was looking over her head, directly at the matron. "I'll have to think about it," he said coolly. "I'll check my calendar and let you know whether I can fit it in."

The matron puffed up like a pigeon and glared at him.

"Young man, only a nobody like you would even consider refusing the committee's invitation to host the Carousel Ball. But then, you wouldn't know anything about what an honor you've been given."

"Inviting him a week beforehand?" Jack Hamilton murmured. "Oh, that's a real honor all right."

Millicent Pendergast obviously wasn't listening. "I told them it wasn't a good idea, making someone who's never before even been eligible to attend into a host." She shook her head at Morganna. "You poor girl. But of course, you got what you deserved, marrying so far beneath your level. You really shouldn't expect someone like him to be able to function in society without a nursemaid."

Morganna reached for Sloan's hand. "Better to be short of experience than of manners," she said clearly.

Millicent Pendergast turned purple. She opened her mouth, closed it, and then spun on her heel and strutted away.

Sloan choked. For a moment his fingers closed tightly on Morganna's, then he let her hand slip out of his as he sank once more into his chair. She glanced once at him and then looked away. He was laughing, of course—as if to say that he found her defense of him as amusing as it was unnecessary. Morganna was annoyed. Didn't he realize that her reason for jumping to his defense wasn't anything personal? She'd have done the same for anyone who was being bullied by Millicent Pendergast.

Jack Hamilton raised his wineglass. "To the Carousel Ball," he said to no one in particular. "For once, it looks as if it might actually be interesting."

CHAPTER FOUR

EMILY glared at her husband. "*Interesting* isn't necessarily the same as *enjoyable,*" she pointed out. "And offending Millicent Pendergast—even though I applaud the sentiment—isn't very wise."

Morganna had to agree with that. She didn't even want to look at her mother. No matter what provocation Millicent had offered, Abigail would probably have a great deal to say about the equal rudeness of Morganna's comment.

"I didn't mean to offend her," Sloan said gently. "I was just buying time to ask you all a simple question. Nobody's ever told me exactly what the duties of a Carousel Ball host are, so how should I know whether I want to do it?"

"Wrong question," Jack said. "No man in his right mind wants to be stuck in that position. That's why the roster of hosts changes every year. Millie and her crew would like you to think it's too much of an honor to let people serve repeatedly, but in fact—"

Morganna stepped in. "There's really nothing much to it. Each host dances once with every debutante, and helps to discreetly arrange other partners in order to make sure none of the girls look like wallflowers. Then at midnight each of the hosts escorts one of the past queens in the grand march—"

"Do I get my choice of queens?"

Sloan's gaze was resting on Morganna with a great deal more warmth than she was accustomed to seeing

60

there. Or, she asked herself uneasily, had the warmth been there all along, but she'd been unable to recognize it because the entire concept seemed so foreign? Until Sloan had made it clear that his long-term plans did not include a platonic marriage, she'd had no reason to be watchful. No reason to wonder what he might be thinking when his gaze happened to fall on her.

"I wouldn't bet my life on it," Jack said. "Millie Pendergast is the one who arranges the grand march."

"But she does it with an eye to what looks best," Abigail put in. "And the two of you, because Sloan is so dark and Morganna so fair, do look wonderful together. So I think, Sloan, if we select your costume to coordinate with Morganna's—which we bought this morning, by the way—even Millicent will have to admit that you should be a couple."

"Costume?" Sloan sounded just short of horrified.

"Nothing elaborate," Abigail said cheerfully. "I was thinking in terms of matching your tuxedo waistcoat and bow tie to her dress, not decking you out as a clown or the Grim Reaper."

"That's all right, then. Just as long as my costume doesn't include tennis balls." The grin Sloan sent at Abigail was loaded with mischievous charm.

"You won't need them, dear," Abigail murmured. "Regardless of how Jack makes it sound, the Carousel Ball isn't boring enough to put anyone to sleep."

"And I suppose now you'd like me to go over to Mrs. Pendergast's table and act humbly grateful for the honor and amenable to my duties. Right, Abigail?"

"No," Abigail said calmly. "Hold off until we've eaten. She put off inviting you to the last minute, after all. It'll do her good to stew in her own juice for a while."

Morganna watched the look of amused sympathy that passed between the two of them, and felt empty inside.

The waiter served their main course, and she picked at her venison steak while she listened to the conversations around her. Abigail was describing Morganna's new ball gown to Emily, and the men had gone back to discussing business.

"I just got the package yesterday," Jack was saying. "I thought you'd fixed that crazy mailing list of yours and finally got my address right, but it was still messed up— so it went across town from your office to mine via our warehouse in Omaha. Of course, they're getting used to it out there and they know where to find me, but still—"

Emily enthused over the dress and said she couldn't wait to see it. "But what I really want to know, Morganna, is what you're planning to donate for the auction at the ball."

At the moment, Morganna couldn't care less. "Just a miniature room."

"Well, of course it's a miniature room," Emily said. "That's what you always do. But what's the theme? I promise not to tell anyone. I think it would be hard to top last year's, myself. That was the dreamiest, sexiest boudoir outside of a fairy princess' castle."

"Auction?" Sloan asked. "Nobody told me anything about an auction. If I'm supposed to stand up in front of a crowd and yodel prices—"

"Don't panic," Emily told him. "The hosts don't have to act as auctioneers, it's completely silent. The money we raise benefits the homeless shelter downtown, and we bring in a good bit—probably because people are feeling just a little guilty about what they've spent on sheer entertainment for the evening."

"Entertainment being a relative term," Jack said under his breath.

Sloan was laughing when a soft buzz from his coat pocket interrupted. "Excuse me," he said and pulled out his cell phone as he moved away from the table.

Morganna heard him say, "Joel? Hang on a minute while I get out of a crowded restaurant. What do you mean, it can't wait?" He stopped in midstep just a couple of yards from the table and went completely silent.

Emily had returned to the question of Morganna's new miniature project. "I bet it's not a bedroom," she said. "That would be too much like the boudoir. Is it even something from a home, or have you finally created the antique shop you said you've always wanted to do?"

Sloan slapped the telephone's antenna back into its slot. "Sorry," he said, his gaze on Morganna. "Joel's over at the factory, and something's wrong. I'm going over. Jack—"

Jack Hamilton got to his feet. "Need a backup, buddy?"

Sloan shook his head. His voice dropped, but Morganna, who was sitting closest, caught part of what he said. "When he pulled up...someone running from the building...thought it was...guys I fired today..."

Jack lifted an eyebrow. "Sure you don't need a hand?"

"No, it's probably nothing. Stay and entertain the ladies. In case I do get tied up, will you see Morganna and Abigail home?"

"My pleasure," Jack said lazily. "How often does a fellow get left with three lovely ladies concentrating only on him?" He pulled out his chair. "Another glass of wine, anyone?"

Morganna wasn't listening. She was trying to remember exactly what Sloan had told Jack earlier about the employees he'd fired. Fragments of the conversation drifted back into her mind, and she wished she'd been listening more closely.

Despite Joel's apparent panic, she told herself, Sloan was no doubt right—this was probably nothing. Of course, he was obliged to take any kind of threat to his business very seriously. But Joel tended to be a worry-wart, and it wouldn't be the first time he'd interrupted Sloan's leisure with something that had turned out to be completely unimportant. Obviously Sloan had remem-bered that, too. If he'd been truly concerned, surely he'd have called for help, or asked Jack to go with him.

And yet she'd watched him stride across the restau-rant—and though he would never have been so rude as to push people out of his way, there had been something in the way he walked which told her he was in enough of a hurry that he'd like to.

It was so hard to keep her mind off what might be going on just a few blocks away at Sticks & Stones that despite her best intentions of keeping her project secret until the auction, she found herself describing the room-box she was building to Emily. "A little boy's room," she said, "completely done in a circus motif. The bed looks like a lion cage on wheels, and there's a music box shaped like a carousel that's less than an inch high and plays that wonderfully tinny music from the circus car-nival."

Emily sighed. "I may have to buy this room."

"You already have two of Morganna's creations," Jack pointed out.

"Not like this one."

Morganna laughed. "Come over for dessert and take a look. Maybe you'll be lucky, Jack, and she'll hate it."

"Or unlucky and she'll insist on building a full-size room onto our house to hold your miniature ones. I know which way I'm betting. But let's go find out," Jack said.

Only then did Morganna realize that she had finished her steak without noticing. The table had been cleared; the coffee cups were empty.

And Sloan had not come back.

While he waited for his car to be brought around, and while he drove the few blocks from the restaurant to Sticks & Stones, Sloan reminded himself of the many times Joel had believed he'd discovered something that required the immediate attention of the boss. Nearly all of them had turned out to be nothing.

It was a shame, Sloan thought, but the fact was that the very qualities which made Joel an invaluable second in command—his attention to detail, his unwillingness to overstep the authority he'd been assigned—were the same things that made it almost impossible that he would ever rise above his current position.

Still, this time there had been a note in Joel's voice that Sloan had never heard there before. What he had seen had scared him, and badly. The man had sounded as if anxiety had crushed his chest till he couldn't get a full breath. And Sloan had to admit, if Joel had indeed seen a pair of recently terminated employees running away from the building, obviously anxious to evade questions, he had good reason for anxiety.

Sloan approached the factory from the back and drove slowly around the block, checking the outside of the building. But he saw nothing unusual, nothing out of place. He noticed that Joel's car was parked well out of the way, half a block down from the factory and across the street—where he would be close enough to observe the front of the building, but far enough away that anyone who was up to mischief probably wouldn't spot him. The car, however, was deserted.

Sloan parked his Jaguar behind Joel's car and started up the street. A flutter from the vacant lot across from the factory caught his attention. During the summer a homeless man had taken up residence on the corner of the lot, behind a sagging picket fence, and resisted all efforts to move him to more appropriate housing. But Sloan hadn't seen him lately; with the weather cooling off, perhaps he'd given in to necessity and gone to a shelter. Which meant that whatever was moving in that vacant lot wasn't necessarily innocent.

But when Sloan checked, the vagrant's spot was empty, without so much as a soda can left behind, and the movement he'd seen turned out to be only a scrap of paper caught in a rogue breeze.

But of course whoever Joel had seen would be long gone by now.

Joel himself was still nowhere to be found. He must have gone inside—but why? What had made him disregard the orders he'd been given to wait for his boss on the sidewalk?

And now what was Sloan to do? He could hardly stroll into the building calling his controller's name. But he didn't want to go skulking in, either, for fear of startling an understandably-edgy Joel and getting clubbed with a half-finished chair leg.

Or what if Joel had blundered in and encountered someone who didn't belong on the property?

Sloan pushed the door open and quickly stepped through and off to one side into the shadows, out of the faint stream of light from the street. He stood quietly for a moment, letting his eyes adjust to the dimness. Then he ran his gaze over the silent silhouettes of the machines that made up the assembly line, the massive rolls of upholstery fabrics and padding, the wooden frames and metal springs and fasteners which stood ready for use.

Far above his head, an impression of movement caught his attention, but by the time he'd focused on the windows of his office, there was nothing to be seen—if indeed there ever had been. A scrap of paper in the vacant lot, a reflection in his office window—Sloan thought wryly that he'd probably start seeing monsters in the dark any minute now.

Everything was silent and at rest—but there was no sense of peace or serenity in the big open space. To Sloan, it seemed instead as if it were waiting.

And then, before he could analyze the feeling, the waiting ended in a split second of sensation that Sloan would remember for the rest of his life.

He watched as his office exploded.

He didn't know if he saw the flash first or felt the concussion, because the two things hit him simultaneously. The fireball assaulted his eyes with brilliant, angry, bluish-red flame, and the shock wave felt as if someone had planted a hand in the center of his chest and given him a solid shove, almost rocking him off his feet.

The room above the factory floor disintegrated, loosing a fine cloud of dust, and an instant later there was a secondary flash as each particle of the powdery, almost century-old dust exploded into flame. He hadn't heard glass shatter, but he saw the shards of his office windows as they fell like crystal raindrops, almost in slow motion, to the factory floor.

And with them, surrounded by the glass, fell something that looked as limp and boneless as a life-size rag doll.

"Oh, no," he whispered. "Joel."

The intense, unearthly light of the double explosion died, leaving behind a flickering and ever-strengthening bluish glow as the flames began to take hold in the paper and old wood that had filled his office. Black smoke rolled out of the now-open room like a boiling thunderhead, crowding against the ceiling but descending inexorably as the cloud expanded.

Joel had fallen between two rolls of fabric. It took Sloan precious seconds to extricate him, to smother the still-glowing spots on what remained of Joel's jacket, and to fling the unconscious man over his shoulder. He had to stop a moment to orient himself before heading toward the door, because stress and exertion were already taking their toll. Though most of the heat was still well above his head, he could feel it beginning to build.

The fiery dust and scraps of the exploded wall had fallen to the production floor, and the hot embers started another host of fires. Each individual blaze was small, but they were growing greedily as they fed on wood and fabric and padding materials. Sloan picked his way between the secondary fires to reach the entrance.

He was staggering under Joel's limp weight by the time he got outside. He paused to gulp cool air and then started across the street to the vacant lot, seeking a safer place to lay his burden down.

A car pulled up. The back door was open before it had stopped, and suddenly Morganna was standing there, staring white-faced at Sloan, at the body that was draped over his shoulder, and then beyond, to where flames licked from the open door and danced behind the still-intact windows at the front of the factory.

"It started in my office," he said hoarsely. His voice sounded all wrong, as if he were talking through a barrel. "Somehow Joel got in the way." Suddenly he started to laugh, a crazy but uncontrollable outburst that horrified him. "Talk about the luck of the draw," he gasped. "We raised the fire insurance just this morning!"

Time seemed to turn into taffy, sometimes drawing out into impossibly long strands, sometimes folding in on itself, compressing and melting together. As long as she lived, Morganna would never be able to correctly piece together the incidents of that evening. Had the fire department trucks roared up first, or the ambulance? Who had finally relieved Sloan of the burden of Joel's unconscious weight? Who had handed her the cup of hot but muddy black coffee? Was it before or after the fire burned through the roof that she had started to shake so violently that they wrapped her in a blanket and made her sit in Jack Hamilton's car? When had the crowds of onlookers begun to gather, and—in a nearly deserted neighborhood—how had they grown so large?

A few episodes stood out, snippets that would be forever singed into her memory. One of them was Jack Hamilton, cell phone to his ear, almost screaming at a dispatcher who he seemed to think was being deliberately obtuse. Another was Morganna's mother putting her arms around Sloan and drawing his head down against her shoulder in a vain attempt to keep him from watching the destruction of his dream.

And the third and perhaps most memorable of all happened as the paramedics started to move the stretcher carrying Joel into the ambulance, and Sloan stepped forward. "Guys, if you can take a second to find his keys, at least we can move his car. It's upwind right now, so it's not in danger, but if the breeze shifts it'll be toast."

"Help yourself," the paramedic said with a shrug.

Gingerly Sloan bent over Joel, who was lying on his

stomach on the stretcher, and reached into his trouser pocket.

Morganna was furious. "How can you even think of something like a stupid car at a time like this?" she snapped.

Sloan pulled back with Joel's key ring in his hand. His eyes were dark with pain. "He loves that car. Right now, the only thing I can do for him is to take care of it. And I owe him, because he did plenty for me."

"What do you mean?"

"Didn't you smell it?"

Morganna wrinkled her nose. "I can smell lots of things at the moment. Smoke, chemicals, fumes. None of them pleasant. If that's what you're talking about—"

A man in fire garb, wearing a helmet that said Investigator, came up to them. "You the owner?"

Sloan shifted his foam cup of coffee and extended a hand. "That's me."

"Mr. Montgomery, do you have any idea who might have wanted to burn your business?"

The question hit Morganna on the raw. "You sound awfully certain that this fire was deliberately set," she said. "Considering that the building is still belching flames, how could you possibly know?"

The investigator looked her over coolly. His gaze seemed to focus on the diamond bracelet peeking out from under the sleeve of her white wool coat. "For one thing, ma'am, the valves appear to be closed on the sprinkler system."

"I wondered why all those expensive sprinkler heads weren't doing any good," Sloan said. "I was going to check, but I was a bit busy at the time, dealing with the injured. Yes, I'm afraid there are a couple of people who might have done this on purpose. When I terminated them just this morning, one said...let me get this right. 'You'll regret this.'"

"Nothing more specific?"

"They didn't invite me to meet them here tonight for a wienie roast, no." Sloan's voice was dry. "When my controller stopped by the factory this evening to pick up some paperwork, he thought he saw one of them—maybe both—running from the building."

"A devoted employee," the investigator observed. "Picking up paperwork at this hour."

"That's Joel." Sloan cleared his throat. "He's very devoted."

"And where is he now? I'd like to talk to him."

Sloan glanced at his watch. "I hope he's in the trauma unit at Nicolet University Hospital."

"He's the one that caught the blast? Where was he when the fire started?"

"In my office. At least, that was where he fell from when the explosion went off."

Morganna began to tremble uncontrollably.

Sloan looked over his shoulder. "Jack," he called. "Take her home, will you?"

"No," Morganna said fiercely. "I'm staying."

Sloan looked at her for a long moment with an unreadable expression in his dark eyes, and then he shrugged. "Have it your own way." He turned back to the fire investigator. "What else can I tell you?"

"Why was he in your office?" the man asked.

"I can't answer that question. He wasn't conscious when I pulled him out, so I couldn't ask him." Sloan's voice cracked just a little. "I don't know what he saw, or heard, or went to look at."

Morganna took a deep breath of the acrid air and moved a little closer to him.

* * *

The eastern sky over Lake Michigan was beginning to pale and streak with light before the fire was under control. For a while, Morganna wasn't certain if the glow she saw was from the coming sunrise or the remnants of the flames reflecting against the smoke-clouded sky.

Even after the flames were knocked down, hot spots continued to smolder, and the raw, throat-slashing smoke hung heavily across the entire warehouse district. In the dim grayness of first light the factory looked bleak. The thick masonry walls still stood, and the heavy beams which had supported the roof were still in place, though some—to her inexperienced eyes—appeared badly charred. Morganna could only imagine what the interior looked like, for fire hoses and yellow safety tape prevented anyone but the fire crews from getting close enough to see.

She wondered what Sloan was thinking. It seemed to be an hour at least since he'd spoken.

Jack Hamilton came up between them, draping one arm over Sloan's shoulders, the other over Morganna's. "I just talked to the hospital again, and Joel's finally stable enough that they'll let you see him for a minute."

Sloan nodded. "I'm on my way. Take Morganna home, will you?"

She shook her head. "No. I'm going with you."

"Morganna, you're exhausted and in shock."

"So are you," she said stubbornly. "And I need to go. It's my responsibility, too." It sounded almost priggish, she thought. But it was true—as the wife of the business's owner, she did have some obligations where Sloan's employees were concerned. And in Joel's case...

I owe Joel a lot more than a hospital visit.

She frowned at the thought, for it was so glaringly obvious that it was scarcely worth considering. Joel had been injured on the job, trying to rescue Sloan's business—so of course she owed him whatever was in her power to do. She had never been particularly fond of Joel, but she'd respected his devotion to his job, and to Sloan.

Perhaps, she admitted, she was even feeling a little guilty for dismissing him as a useless worrier—because this time he'd so obviously been right.

She looked around, feeling as if she was beginning to come out of a daze. "Where's Mother?"

"Emily took her home a couple of hours ago," Sloan said. "That was the other time you refused to leave. They took Joel's car, in case you're wondering where it went."

"Are you sure you're okay to drive, Sloan?" Jack asked. "Morganna's right about you being in shock. I'll take you if you like."

Sloan shook his head. "I'd rather you stay here and keep an eye on things a little longer—if you can. Where'd you park my car?"

Jack pointed. "About three blocks that way. I figured if I took it any further, you'd probably come back to find the wheels gone, but if I stayed any closer the embers might fry the paint."

"Good thinking. The last thing I need is to have to deal with the car insurance people, too." Sloan glanced down at Morganna's high-heeled shoes. "It's going to be a hike."

Morganna shrugged. "So? If I'd known the evening's entertainment included a barbecue, I'd have dressed more appropriately. But since I've already been standing for hours, what's a few blocks to walk?"

She didn't realize until she started walking that she was cold to the bone, so chilled that her muscles were stiff. She even stumbled a couple of times on uneven spots in the sidewalk. They'd gone less than half a block when Sloan muttered something under his breath, then reached for her hand and tucked it tightly into the bend of his elbow. Automatically Morganna drew as far away as his grip would allow her to.

Sloan's voice was chilly. "If you think I'm making some kind of move on you, Morganna, let me assure you that right now, I couldn't possibly be less in the mood for making love."

She bit her tongue hard, and when she regained her self-control she said acidly, "And here I thought that all the girls would be wearing *eau de smoke* next season because men find it such a turn-on."

"I'll keep the possibility in mind. Since it's apparent that I'm not going to be making furniture again anytime soon, I may be looking for another line of work, and a hot new perfume might be just the ticket. We've certainly got the raw materials to work with."

Even though she had stood and watched the factory burn, she hadn't yet considered the possibility that the fire might actually put him out of business. "But the insurance...you can rebuild, Sloan."

"Eventually, yes. But it's not going to be any quick process." He helped her into the Jaguar. "You don't have to come into the trauma unit with me."

"I want to be there."

He started the car. "I didn't realize you were so attached to Joel."

She didn't bother to answer. If he didn't understand her reasons, she couldn't possibly explain them. And they were both so tired now that a single misspoken word could lead to a massive quarrel.

Except, of course, for the fact that they had never quarreled.

Morganna hadn't really thought about that before. If

anything, she had considered the absence of arguments as one of the few blessings of her marriage. But once she stopped to consider the situation, the reason quickly became clear. There had to be a certain level of communication—the desire to express a conviction or share a concern or change the other person's mind—in order to quarrel. Without that, a couple might snipe sarcastically at each other, but they couldn't work up a good verbal battle.

She was definitely worn out, she told herself, if she was actually wishing for an old-fashioned argument. A rousing, roof-raising, clear-the-air kind of fight…

In the brightly lit hospital corridor, staff members wrinkled their noses or drew aside as they passed. Morganna happened to glance down at her once-white wool coat, and for the first time saw the streaks of soot which had turned it a mangy-looking gray. If the two of them smelled as bad as she must look, no wonder people were going out of their way to avoid encountering them.

Just inside the trauma unit, she stood a few steps from the desk and waited while Sloan talked to the staff. The nurse who seemed to be in charge shook her head firmly and raised her voice. "We can let you look through the window into his cubicle, Mr. Montgomery, but that's all. There's no point in going in, anyway."

Morganna tried to swallow her horror. No point? Was he dying, then?

"Why?" Sloan asked baldly.

"Because though he's stable for the moment, he's unresponsive. Between the burns, the surgery he needed to set his broken leg, and the fall he took, he's on massive doses of painkillers, and it'll probably be several days before anyone can talk to him. Even then, he won't be talking back right away. He's on a ventilator to assist his breathing, because of the hot gases he inhaled.''

"But he's going to be all right eventually?"

The nurse hesitated. "You should talk to his doctors to get the official word. But he'll definitely be scarred. And it could be days before we know exactly how much damage the fire did to his lungs."

Sloan rubbed the back of his neck as if it hurt. "He's to have everything he needs."

The nurse's voice gentled. "If you'll leave your phone number, I'll ask his staff doctor to call you after rounds in the morning." She showed them to the window, and they stood there for a few minutes, looking at the almost-unrecognizable form in the bed. It wasn't until Morganna started to turn away from the window that she realized her hand was cupped in Sloan's, and she wasted a moment wondering how it had gotten there.

"Save his clothes," Sloan told the nurse. "The fire investigator will want them."

In the corridor once more, Morganna said, "What's important about his clothes? They must have destroyed everything, just getting it off him."

"It's not the fabric, it's what's on it."

She frowned.

"Gasoline," Sloan said softly. "It splashed on Joel's jacket, but—thank heaven—it didn't all burn, or he'd be a great deal worse off right now."

"Gasoline?" Her voice felt very small.

He stopped in the center of the hall and looked down at her. Something in his gaze was oddly gentle. "You don't think my office exploded for no reason, do you? Morganna, that room was laced with gasoline. And it was intended for me."

CHAPTER FIVE

MORGANNA had held up through the initial horror of the fire because the shock had numbed her to what she was watching. She'd held up through the long smoky hours that followed because at any given time she'd simply refused to look beyond the next minute. She'd held up outside Joel's hospital room, looking at a very badly injured man, because she'd forced herself to believe that he would be absolutely all right.

She wasn't sure she was going to make it through Sloan's announcement.

It was intended for me, he had said very matter-of-factly. Someone had filled his office with gasoline as a booby trap for him. Someone had intended it to blow up in his face. Someone had intended it to be Sloan who was lying in the trauma unit now.

Or in the morgue.

She saw the air around her start to turn faintly orange, and with her last shred of self-control she grabbed for Sloan's arm. He pushed her into the nearest waiting area and into a chair, forcing her head down till the blood flowed back where it belonged. She sat there taking deep breaths for several minutes. "I'm all right," she said finally, and though he looked as if he had his doubts, he offered his arm. This time she leaned gratefully on him as they walked across the pedestrian bridge from the hospital complex to the parking garage.

"Thanks," she said gruffly without looking at him. "You've got enough to deal with right now without me going woozy on you. I suppose I should have gone home the first time you asked me to.''

"Not much point in fussing about it now," he said. He unlocked the car and opened her door. "But I'm glad you didn't.''

He said it so quietly that she wasn't even certain she'd heard right, and by the time he'd walked around the car and gotten behind the wheel, any trace of sentiment was gone from his voice. "Why were you even there, Morganna? I thought you'd be at the restaurant for another hour.''

She shrugged. "Nobody seemed in any mood to linger. When you hadn't come back by the time we finished dinner, I asked Jack to drive by Sticks & Stones, just to see if you were still there and if there was anything we could do.'' And how carefully casual she had been with that request, she recalled. She had phrased it as nothing more than idle curiosity, for she'd rather have had her fingernails pulled out than admit to what had seemed at the time to be completely irrational concern for Sloan. She even remembered wondering if Sloan might think she was trying to spy on him. "We must have still been too far away to hear the blast.''

"There wasn't one, really. At least, not a blast like a bomb going off. It was more like a dull thud than a sharp crack.''

"Oh. I would have thought... Then when we pulled up in front, you were stumbling out the door, and there was fire behind you—'' She had started to shiver again. "And Joel's clothes were smoldering—''

He didn't look at her. "I'll do everything I can for him, Morganna.''

She was startled. Did he honestly think she needed

reassurance on that point? Of course he wouldn't do anything less.

At this hour of the morning, the six square blocks which formed Pemberton Place, Lakemont's most exclusive neighborhood, were almost entirely quiet and dark. The exception was the Georgian mansion which sat almost squarely in the center of the district. There, the main-floor lights blazed in brilliant contrast to the still-faint glow of daylight, and the front door opened as the car pulled into the circular driveway.

Morganna got out. She was startled when Sloan killed the engine and followed her up the front steps instead of taking the Jaguar around to the garage.

Selby was at the door. "I'm so sorry, sir," he murmured. "Mrs. Ashworth told the staff what happened. What can I get for you?"

Sloan glanced at Morganna. "A little brandy wouldn't be a bad idea. Mrs. Montgomery has had a shock."

"Indeed, sir." The butler silently vanished down the hall.

Sloan glanced into the silent drawing room. "I suppose Selby thought it would be a bit redundant to greet us with a fire, but you're still shivering."

Morganna shook her head. "Don't light it for me. All I want is to have a shower and fall into bed. Besides, if we sit down in there, the smoke will get into the upholstery—and if you're not going to be building furniture for a while, then we need to take very good care of what we already have."

The joke felt as feeble as it must have sounded; Sloan didn't laugh.

"Sorry. I was only trying... Never mind." She turned toward the stairway just as Selby came from the back of the house with a decanter and two glasses on a tray. "Is my mother asleep, Selby?"

"I doubt it, Miss Morganna. She asked me to let her know when you got home."

"Don't bother. I'll tap on her door." She stopped at the base of the stairs, looking back at Sloan. Somewhere inside the tired and half-empty pit where her brain used to be, a thought nudged at her. He had lost so much tonight, she told herself. She should do something to comfort him. The problem was, she didn't even know how to begin. Her mother would have simply walked over and put her arms around him....

Before she could act, Sloan picked up one of the glasses from Selby's tray and went into the drawing room, closing the door behind him.

Morganna climbed the stairs.

Sloan had scrubbed till his skin ached, trying to wash away the stink of the fire. But the smoke must have crept deep into his lungs where he couldn't wash, for he could still smell it after his shower.

And as long as the smell was there, he couldn't put the rest of the evening's events out of his mind, either.

As soon as he closed his eyes, he relived it all in slow motion. The first brilliant flash of light, the feeling of being shoved hard, the secondary explosion of the dust which had been shaken loose by the initial tremor.

And then, inevitably, seeing Joel fall. Sloan had no doubt that he'd be watching that scene in his nightmares for years to come.

Abruptly he sat up and tapped the bedside lamp to turn it on, and piled the pillows into a stack against his back.

What made the memory of that fall even worse was the knowledge that Joel had been only a bystander, not the intended target. But it wasn't some sick sense of relief for himself that Sloan was feeling. Instead there was an irrational whisper in the back of his mind, saying that Joel should not have been there at all, that Sloan should have been doing his own checking.

It was a completely illogical accusation, of course, for he'd very specifically told Joel to wait for him outside. But logic—and even truth—were seldom effective at banishing guilt.

Who hates me enough to do that?

The workers he'd fired that morning, of course. The answer was just about as obvious as it could be. There had been a gleam of satisfaction in the fire investigator's eyes when he'd heard the details about those workers. The job termination, the threat, the fact that Joel had seen at least one of them on the premises just minutes before the fire started. Open-and-shut case.

They'd gotten even all right, exactly as they'd intended. Sloan would be paying the price for a long time to come. But what they obviously hadn't considered was that their friends and fellow workers would pay as well, by being put out of work. And in the end, the arsonists themselves wouldn't feel much glee over their triumph when they ended up sitting in a jail cell, as they surely would, with nothing to do but think.

Burning down the factory had been a useless, pointless, stupid thing to do. *Obviously,* Sloan thought, *we aren't dealing with a pair of Rhodes scholars here.*

But the reasons didn't matter now; that was the job of the fire investigator. The damage was done and now the problem lay in how best to fix it. First thing tomorrow, he'd have to call the insurance company. And then the next task would be to find a construction engineer who could tell him whether the building could be salvaged, and an architect who could take on the job of reconstructing the old factory or designing a new one. Then he might be able to tell his workers how long they could expect to be idle....

But all those things would have to wait until after he'd checked on Joel and talked to the doctors.

He slapped at the lamp to turn it off and closed his eyes, fully expecting to see the explosion again. But this time it was Morganna's face he saw in the darkness instead, her eyes wide with dread as she stared through the trauma unit window at Joel's motionless body. He wondered what, exactly, she had been thinking right then. She'd been so absorbed she hadn't even noticed when he'd taken her hand. Not that the horror of Joel's injuries wouldn't have been enough to shock her—but had she been picturing Sloan himself lying in that bed?

Probably not, he told himself. At that point, she might not even have considered the possibility that it could have been Sloan who was injured.

He had to hand it to her, because she'd taken the whole thing like a trouper—at least, right up until he'd told her about the gasoline trap. He hadn't been thinking clearly himself by then, or he'd have realized it was just a little too much, expecting her to take that in stride. Still, he hadn't anticipated that she'd faint. She wasn't the fainting sort; she'd only done it a couple of times in her life.

At least, that was all he knew about. And of course he'd been the cause of both those episodes....

Had she simply reached the end of her rope at that point? Or had she been truly shaken at the thought that he might have been seriously—even fatally—hurt?

Wishful thinking, Montgomery. You've just got Morganna on your mind tonight—for all the usual reasons.

What would have happened if he'd asked her to come upstairs with him? To spend what remained of the night with him?

Why was he even wasting time thinking about it? She'd have given him the sharp side of her tongue, that was for sure. And with good reason, for he'd told her himself he wasn't in the mood for making love.

At the instant he'd said it, it had been true enough. But then she'd snapped at him about the aroma of smoke being an aphrodisiac, and damned if he hadn't looked down at her—streaked with soot, hair falling down, eyes reddened by fumes and unshed tears, smelling of fire— and almost staggered under the sudden desire to take her straight to bed.

And he still wanted her now—there was no doubt about that. But the truth was, whether they made love or not, he'd give anything not to have to face the night alone.

If he were to cross the hall and tap on her door and tell her that...

"She'd hand you a teddy bear," he told himself crossly. He scattered the stack of pillows and let his head drop back against his favorite one.

And saw his office explode into flame once more.

He wondered if he would ever again close his eyes and *not* see it.

Morganna was scarcely awake the next morning before her feet were on the floor and she was reaching for a sweater and a pair of jeans. There were too many questions in her mind to allow her to stay quietly in bed, and the mere thought of a solitary breakfast tray made her feel ill.

The butler was just laying a hand on the dining-room

doorknob when she reached the bottom of the stairs. "Selby," she called, "is my mother in there?"

He turned hastily, looking horrified to see her already dressed and downstairs. "Miss Morganna, I didn't realize you'd be awake so early. You should have rung for your tray."

"I don't want it."

"I see," he said. "Yes, Mrs. Ashworth is in the dining room. There's an assortment of food on the sideboard, but would you like me to bring your usual breakfast in?"

She took a closer look. Selby seemed ten years older this morning, almost haggard. "For heaven's sake, Selby, I can take care of myself. You didn't have any more sleep last night than the rest of us did. Go have a nap."

"Yes, miss."

Morganna didn't believe for an instant that he would actually take himself off duty, but at least she'd tried. She let him open the dining-room door for her.

Abigail was indeed in the room, with a cup of coffee, a concerned frown on her face and Sloan sitting next to her.

Selby really is tired, Morganna thought. He'd forgotten to warn her of Sloan's whereabouts. He usually did so almost automatically, without her needing to ask. It had become something of a conspiracy between them, over the months.

Not that it would have mattered this morning, of course. If Sloan hadn't been in the dining room, she'd have had to go looking for him. As he started to stand up, Morganna waved him back into his chair and asked briskly, "How's Joel this morning?"

"About the same," Sloan said.

Morganna turned from the sideboard with a cup and saucer and caught her mother's gaze. Abigail was watching her closely, her eyes narrowed. Then she looked deliberately from Morganna to Sloan.

Oops, Morganna thought. In all the stress, she'd forgotten for a moment that under these circumstances, the loving wife she was supposed to be would have greeted her husband before asking even the most important questions. And it didn't look as if Abigail was likely to assume that Morganna and Sloan had already said hello over the toothpaste—so some sort of gesture seemed necessary. The quicker and more casual the better, she decided, so even if he was startled Abigail wouldn't have time to notice.

Morganna leaned over the back of Sloan's chair to give him a one-armed hug, pressing her cheek briefly against his, intending to pull back almost instantly. But instead, his hand came up to capture hers and hold it firmly against his chest. She could feel his heart beating steadily under her fingertips, and her own skittering madly as he turned his head and kissed the corner of her mouth. The saucer she was holding trembled, and the cup rattled a warning.

With what must have looked like great reluctance, Sloan released her, and Morganna sank into a chair.

Abigail reached for the coffeepot, which stood at her elbow. "Good thing you hadn't already filled that cup," she murmured. "Did I forget to mention that you shouldn't be shy about expressing your affections in front of me?"

Selby came quietly into the room. "Mr. Montgomery, the fire investigator is here, requesting to see you."

Sloan looked at Abigail. "You were wondering what he's like—now you can see for yourself. Show him in, please, Selby."

This morning, without the heavy fireman's coat and

boots and helmet, the investigator looked much more approachable, but Morganna noticed the way his gaze swept over the room when he came in. She would have sworn there wasn't a single item he'd missed.

"Coffee?" Sloan asked. "You met my wife last night. This is her mother, Mrs. Ashworth."

The investigator nodded at Morganna, shook Abigail's hand, and took the cup Selby offered. "Thanks. This looks much better than the stuff we were drinking last night. You have a nice place here, Mr. Montgomery."

"Thank you," Sloan said. "The house has belonged to my wife's family for over a century."

"I see." The investigator's gaze slid meditatively over Morganna's face. "I thought you might like to know what we've turned up so far. I have only very preliminary findings as yet, of course. It could take days, maybe weeks, before we have all the results of lab tests and everything."

"Weeks?" Sloan sounded less than pleased. "When can I get onto the premises with a construction engineer to find out exactly how bad the damage is?"

The investigator's eyes were bright. "You're going to rebuild?"

"That's what the construction engineer is for—to tell me whether it's financially feasible. Or even possible."

"Of course. Well, you can go in today if you like. As long as you go with me."

Morganna said, "I don't think that's such a good idea, Sloan. The building might not be stable—"

"I've got an extra helmet in my car," the investigator said casually.

She was irritated. "Oh, that would do a lot of good if one of the walls collapsed!"

"I won't take him anywhere he won't be safe, ma'am."

Which puts me pretty firmly in my place, Morganna thought. Sloan looked a little annoyed, too—as if he thought she was being overprotective. So she bit her tongue.

The investigator turned to Sloan. "In fact, Mr. Montgomery, I'd like very much for you to come with me today. I hope you can tell us what was already there in the building, and what may have been brought in to start or feed the fire."

"I can already tell you one thing that wasn't there when I left yesterday. I don't store gasoline in my office."

The investigator raised an eyebrow. "How did you know there was gasoline, Mr. Montgomery?"

"I smelled it on Joel's clothes when I carried him out. It was pretty obvious."

"Yeah," the investigator said casually, "it is hard to miss, isn't it? People think gasoline burns up entirely and leaves no trace, but it's one of the easiest things in the world to spot. There doesn't seem to be any kind of container, though. I suppose our arsonist could be the tidy sort, and he carried the gas can out with him. Though they usually don't, since it doubles the chances of being spotted with the evidence. Tell me about that natural gas space heater beside your desk, Mr. Montgomery. Did you leave it turned on or off yesterday?"

"Off, of course. I only used it on very cold mornings and never if I was away from the office for more than a few minutes. Why?"

"Because it was burning like a blowtorch last night till the crews got the gas switched off at the main."

"I suppose the explosion could have broken something," Sloan offered.

The investigator shook his head. "Nope. The natural gas had to be leaking already when the spark hit. That was what blew the place up, because there simply wasn't enough gasoline to have exploded like that. And none of the fittings were broken. I looked this morning."

Morganna's fingers tightened on her cup. "But how on earth do you know all that? The building's in shambles!"

"You'd be surprised what we can figure out," the investigator said easily. "It takes us days sometimes to get to the bottom of the debris, but we get there eventually. We're looking for what's there but isn't supposed to be—like gas cans. And also we're looking for what's supposed to be there but isn't."

She frowned. "I don't understand. If something isn't there, how can you possibly know that it's missing?"

"It's mostly common sense. We look for valuables. Important papers. Photo albums. Family pets. Those are all things people don't want to lose in a fire, so sometimes they remove them before the fire starts."

"But if they know there's going to be a fire..." Her voice trailed off. "I see. If they knew, then they're automatically guilty of the arson."

"Something like that." The investigator drained his coffee cup. "If you're ready, Mr. Montgomery, let's go take a look at your building."

Be careful, Morganna wanted to say. But it would probably only earn her another impatient look from Sloan and a condescending comment from the investigator.

She hoped the investigator wouldn't notice that there was no photograph of her mixed in with whatever was left of Sloan's desk. In fact, he'd never displayed one—

but she'd hate for the investigator to get the wrong idea about why something which common sense said should be there so obviously wasn't.

A fire engine still stood in the street outside, with a skeleton crew standing by, on the lookout for flare-ups and hot spots. The investigator nodded to them and passed on by. Sloan took a deep breath and followed.

The sight of the interior of his factory, shattered and blackened, with one corner of the roof open to the sky, turned Sloan's stomach. He picked his way across the production floor in the fire investigator's wake. Yesterday, he could have walked across the enormous room blindfolded and not even stubbed his toe, because he knew every inch of his property so well. Today, even if all the debris had been magically whisked away, he'd have had trouble, because everything looked different. Even the machines, which weren't obviously ruined, looked alien because of the oily soot that coated every surface.

"Not much point in paying a construction engineer to state the obvious," he said, almost to himself.

"The obvious? You mean that it's not worth salvaging?" The investigator kicked at a lump of debris.

"That's what it looks like to me."

"I've seen worse. The building is pretty solid, and once all the mess is cleaned up it'll look a lot different. But I guess I wouldn't blame you for taking the insurance money and retiring. Playing billiards, or whatever it is you do in that big house."

"I'm a little young to retire to billiards," Sloan said curtly. "I was just thinking that it might be more practical to start over somewhere else."

"Wait and see. At least the roof beams are still solid.

If they'd been steel, they'd have twisted like spaghetti when the water hit them.'' He stopped and kicked at a blackened length of wood. ''Do you notice anything out of place?''

Sloan stared at him for a second, then said dryly, ''I assume you're not talking about the obvious. No, I don't see anything that shouldn't be here. Or anything missing, either.''

''Then let's very carefully go upstairs to your office and take a look.'' The investigator added casually, ''Your wife doesn't seem to want me to look very closely at this fire.''

Sloan's gut tightened. ''What do you mean by that?''

''Just a feeling. She seemed to be making the implication that I don't know what I'm talking about when it comes to things like whether a natural gas connection is open, and whether a sprinkler system has been deliberately shut off.''

Sloan shrugged. He hoped the gesture looked more natural than it felt. ''She's a novice at fires, and especially at understanding arson. I was curious about those things, too.''

''I see. Well, I'm just doing my job. And part of my job is, whenever somebody tries to discourage me from looking, I look a little harder. Now, Mr. Montgomery— what do you see?''

Morganna turned the circus-theme room box around on the rotating stand on her worktable and looked into it through the tiny windows. A six-inch-tall window-peeker would be quite impressed, she thought. The lion-cage bed was particularly striking, and she was very pleased with how easy it had been to convert the design for a carnival popcorn cart into a small desk, complete with a tiny lamp with a real bulb built into the striped canopy on top.

The room box was nearly done, ahead of schedule for the Carousel Ball auction. Of course, that was largely because she hadn't moved from her worktable all day. She felt just a little guilty about that, and especially about leaving her mother to entertain herself for hours on end. But it would have done no good to pace the floor and fret, which was what Abigail seemed to want her to do. Instead Morganna had kept her hands busy with something useful, and as usual, she found that the physical work concentrated her mind as well.

And of course, her mother would have been welcome to join her. In fact, Abigail had been in and out of the workroom several times during the day. At midafternoon, she'd come in to report that Sloan still hadn't returned, and when Morganna merely shrugged and said she wasn't surprised, Abigail had given a snort and asked if Morganna ever paid attention to anything that was larger than dollhouse scale.

"Miniatures are my hobby, Mother," she'd said quietly.

"No, Morganna, they've become an obsession. Letting them take over this room was one thing. Allowing them to take over your life is another."

And perhaps, Morganna thought wearily, Abigail was right. It was so much easier to retreat to the miniature room than it was to spar with Sloan, or to perform the role of happy wife for her friends. Emily Hamilton understood, of course—but she was the only one Morganna had confided in. And even Emily didn't know all the details.

She picked up the tiny circus train which she had so

laboriously fabricated, and set it on a track that circled the room just below ceiling level.

Behind her, Sloan said, "That train would make any real little boy drool. And maybe a few big boys, too."

She hadn't heard him come in. She straightened a stuffed animal in the pile atop the lion-cage bed. "Are you talking about yourself? I didn't know you were a model train buff, Sloan."

"There's a lot you don't know about me." His tone was matter-of-fact.

Morganna bit her lip. "How did it go today—with the investigator?"

"Nasty." He pulled up a stool and perched beside her. "That room is really beautiful."

Morganna eyed it critically. "Do you think it's too neat and orderly? For a little boy's room, I mean."

"Maybe. It also looks a little chilly, with nobody there to enjoy all those great toys. Why don't you ever put people in your scenes?"

"Because I've never found ones that look real enough. Nothing ruins a miniature fantasy faster than a stiff plastic-looking doll in the middle of it. So I pretend that the people have just stepped out." She pushed back from the table and looked at him levelly. "What happened today that you don't want to talk about?"

For a moment, she thought he wasn't going to answer. "The insurance company investigator showed up. It's going to be a mess, Morganna. Because it's definitely arson, the company is very reluctant to pay the claim until there's a suspect in jail. And the fact that I increased the coverage just this week didn't help my credibility with either the insurance guy or the fire investigator."

The sensation of déjà vu swept over her. Time seemed to fold in on itself as she relived the announcement that her father's suicide meant that the life insurance company was *reluctant to pay the claim...*

But eventually that had all worked out, she reminded herself. At least, Sloan had told her that it had, and she tried to smother the lingering doubt that he'd actually funded that check for Abigail himself. It had turned out all right before. So surely this time, too—

"You mean they haven't arrested those men yet?" she asked.

"No. And they probably won't for a while."

She frowned. "Why not?"

"All kinds of reasons, apparently. Mostly because they want to be absolutely certain of getting a conviction. You heard the investigator this morning, about taking a while to get all the test results. And until they can talk to Joel—"

"How much evidence does it take?"

"More than they have at the moment, obviously." He took a deep breath. "I've just talked to your mother, Morganna. I've asked her to go back to Arizona immediately."

"What?" She was stunned. "Sloan, you can't just kick my mother out of the house! And why would you want to get rid of her, for heaven's sake?"

"Because I want you to go with her."

She stared at him. "Why?"

"Use your head, honey. The guys who burned the factory didn't accomplish everything they set out to do."

"You mean," she said coolly, "that they didn't succeed in turning you into a cinder. And you're afraid they'll try again."

"No," he corrected. "I'm afraid if they do try again, they might miss and get you instead."

Morganna was startled at the warmth that flooded over

her. She hadn't anticipated feeling so good about the idea that he wanted to protect her.

"Or they might hurt Abigail by mistake," he added. "And I already feel guilty enough about Joel."

The warmth receded as quickly as it had come. So he classified his wife in precisely the same category as he put his mother-in-law, she told herself bitterly. And his controller. Well, what else had she expected?

"You're right," she said. "Up to a point. In fact, I'll take Mother to the airport myself. But I'm not going with her."

"Your devotion to duty is charming, Morganna. But please do me a favor and stop short of declaring that your place is beside me, facing whatever comes our way. I'm already feeling a little ill today and I'm not sure I could stomach that cliché."

She pulled back as if she'd been slapped.

Sloan rubbed the back of his neck. "Okay, I probably shouldn't have said that."

"Really? I thought you were trying to make me mad enough to get on a plane. And that comment came pretty close."

"On the other hand, if it works…" he muttered.

"But not close enough. I am not leaving. Is that clear?"

"Dammit, Morganna, why not?"

Because my place is beside you, facing whatever comes our way. The words seemed to echo through her head.

It was a cliché, he was right about that. But there was a reason that sayings grew into proverbs—it was because they were true.

And in this case, it wasn't Morganna's sense of duty that had made those words come to her mind. It was far more than that. Heaven help her, she *wanted* to be beside him, sharing good and bad, laughter and tears. Sharing everything.

Exactly when, she wondered miserably, had she made the gigantic mistake of falling in love with a man who wanted only a trophy for a wife?

CHAPTER SIX

MORGANNA had thought there could be nothing more destructive to a woman's pride than being married to a man she didn't love. Now she knew there was something infinitely worse—loving a man who wanted her only as a decoration for his life, not as a real part of it.

Even his invitation to make their marriage a physical union as well as a legal one had been nothing more than an extension of the role he had assigned her as trophy wife. He wanted her in his bed because their children would be one more visible sign of his success. And because sleeping with her would be convenient for him, and no doubt pleasant enough. But he hadn't invited her into his bedroom because he felt any particular tenderness for Morganna. Any other woman with the same social background would have done as well.

She was absolutely furious with herself. How could she have been such a fool as to overlook all that and fall in love with him anyway?

For six months she had resented both Sloan and the circumstances that had forced her to accept the reality of being his wife. Or at least, she had believed that was what she was resenting. Now it was becoming painfully apparent that somewhere since their marriage her thinking had shifted, so slowly and subtly that she hadn't even felt the disparity creeping up on her.

Why it had happened, she had no idea. Was she really so shallow that his lavish gifts—the designer dresses and diamond bracelets she had told herself she detested—had purchased her loyalty anyway? Surely not, because what she was feeling was not calculated fondness for a sugar daddy who could provide her with expensive toys that her friends would envy. It was an aching hunger for a soul mate—for the one man in the world who could complete her, who could truly be her other half. The man who could love her as much as she loved him, and who wanted to join with her in a union—an emotional and spiritual bonding as well as a physical one—that would grow closer and deeper and more intense with the passing years.

Unfortunately, when she had selected the man she wanted to be her soul mate, she hadn't chosen very wisely. It was not a role Sloan would be able to understand, much less one that he would find attractive.

The oddest thing was the fact that admitting she loved him—though it had rocked her emotionally—had left everything else essentially unchanged. A couple of days ago Morganna had refused to go to bed with a man she didn't love. Now that objection was gone, but nothing else had truly altered. So long as Sloan looked at her as nothing more than a convenience—a trophy—she could not act on her love. He had made very clear what it was he expected of her, and the last thing she could do was to change the rules. She couldn't even tell him what she wanted, because the very thought of admitting her desires and then seeing him look at her with distaste or revulsion was more than she could bear.

"I guess I'm not surprised," Sloan said, "that you're having to search pretty hard for an answer that will justify your stubbornness."

Answer? Morganna had to fumble through her shell-shocked memory just to find the question. Why wouldn't

she leave, that was it. "This is my home," she said
stiffly.

"If that's the best you can do—" Sloan held up both
hands in a gesture of surrender. "All right. You win.
Stay."

He strode across the room, frustration showing in
every line of his body.

Morganna braced her elbows on the edge of her worktable and put her face down in her hands. She'd won the
battle, for what it was worth. Regardless of what Sloan
thought, she was staying right where her heart, as well
as her principles, said she belonged. Beside him.

She just wished that he actually wanted her to be there.

After dinner, Sloan went to the hospital to check on Joel,
and Abigail retreated to the library to make a telephone
call. With the evening looming long ahead of her,
Morganna climbed the stairs to change out of her dinner
dress. She was sitting at her dressing table in a raspberry-
colored satin robe, toying with a perfume atomizer, when
Abigail knocked on the door.

"I just wanted to tell you," Abigail said, "that I'm
glad you're not leaving, Morganna. I'm not pleased to
have you in danger, of course, and I don't think Sloan is
the sort to get panicky about your safety for no reason.
Still, I'm very proud that you feel your place is with your
husband, no matter what."

Morganna's throat was too tight to speak.

Abigail fiddled with a cobalt-blue bottle of moisturiz-
ing lotion. "And I also came to tell you that I think
perhaps I should stay, too."

Morganna's hand convulsively clutched the atomizer,
drenching the lapel of her robe with perfume. "You're
not going back to Phoenix? But why not? If your admirer

hasn't given up his obsession quite yet, maybe you'd like to try Florida for a while. Or southern California. There are a lot of other places besides here and Phoenix.''

"It begins to sound as if you'd like to see the back of me," Abigail said gently.

Morganna's eyes widened. "Of course not." But even to her own ears, her protest was unconvincing. She tried again. "I couldn't bear it if you stayed here out of a misguided sense of loyalty and something happened to you, Mother."

"You surely don't expect me to run away to safety and leave you. Do you, Morganna?"

"But we're fine. Sloan and I—" Her voice almost cracked on the words. "We have each other, and—"

"No, you're not fine," Abigail said firmly. "And you don't have each other. Where you and Sloan are concerned, there is no *we*."

Morganna focused on a fingerprint that marred the glass surface of her dressing table and reached for a tissue to rub it off. "I don't know what you're talking about, Mother."

"Oh, honey, it's time for a little truth. Do you think I haven't known all along what you did? The bargain you made?"

Morganna stared at her, unbelieving. *And you let me do it?*

"I suppose I saw what I wanted to see," Abigail said slowly. "But I believed—I honestly believed—that it would be all right. Sloan was so touchingly eager to help—I thought that could only mean that he was head over heels in love with you. And as for you, Morganna— I thought it was impossible for you to look at the way he'd thrown himself so selflessly into the mess your father left and not fall in love with him. I thought your haste only anticipated what would have happened anyway.''

''And if I was going to end up married to him sooner or later, why not make the most of Sloan's willingness to be a knight in shining armor at the moment we needed him?'' Morganna's voice was hollow.

''That's not a very flattering way to put it, though I suppose you're right. What I didn't expect was how difficult it would be to build this marriage. How much extra pressure you both were under because of rushing into things as you did. I guess I supposed the tension would all melt away because of the power of love.''

It might have, Morganna thought, *if there had been any love to warm things up.*

''At first, whenever I called, you just sounded stressed. And of course there was plenty of reason for strain, so I kept telling myself that as things settled down, you and Sloan would find your way together. But lately, no matter how hard you've tried to sound happy, the bitterness has been there underneath. And it's been growing. So I came back to Lakemont to see for myself what was going on.''

Morganna's eyes were stinging with tears of embarrassment and pain. She wondered if Abigail had been amused or merely annoyed by the show they'd tried so hard to put on for her.

''It's breaking my heart, darling, to see the barrier that's grown up between you two because of pride and wounded self-esteem and uncertainty. I'm sure down deep you each know you did the right thing—but it's only human to be just a little fearful that the other one regrets making such a hasty decision. And where there are doubts—even baseless ones—it's very difficult to build trust.''

Morganna blinked in surprise. That sentimental nonsense made it sound almost as if Abigail hadn't seen through their performance after all. That she'd thought the touches and kisses and hugs were sincere, and any tension that showed between them was simply because of their questions and their pride. Had she honestly seen only half the picture?

My mother the romantic, Morganna thought wryly. *Of course, she also thought that it was a good idea to trust my father to take care of the family finances....*

"But there's one thing I know," Abigail said firmly. "No matter how insurmountable the wall between you looks, Morganna, it can be removed. It went up one small block at a time, and it can be torn down the same way. That's why I'm so glad you refused to leave today, because right now Sloan needs you. And this is your best chance to break down that barricade between you."

She'd half expected to resent the string of platitudes, but instead Morganna felt a wave of gratitude surge over her. Though Abigail had turned out to be more perceptive than Morganna had hoped she'd be, thank heaven she hadn't shed the rose-colored glasses entirely. How much worse it would be if Abigail realized the truth! If she actually understood how impossible it was that their cold-blooded bargain could ever metamorphose into a happy marriage, she'd torture herself with guilt for not stopping it in the first place. And she'd probably start selling her belongings on the street to try to repay Sloan every last dime he'd spent on either of them.

A tap on the door interrupted. "Morganna?" Sloan called softly.

If he'd known Abigail was inside, Morganna thought, he wouldn't have knocked, much less waited for permission. He'd have strolled in as if he did so half a dozen times a day. But only after Morganna answered did he enter.

He smiled at Abigail, who offered her cheek to be kissed, and then came to stand behind Morganna at the dressing table. His hands rested on her shoulders, his fingertips lightly massaging the taut muscles. The thin satin seemed to melt away under his touch, and Morganna felt heat rush all the way to her toes.

He lifted the mass of hair and stooped to kiss her nape. "Honey, maybe it's because of all the smoke last night, but your sense of smell seems to be a little off. Your robe seems to have been laundered in Midnight Passion instead of water."

She thought about picking up the perfume atomizer she'd accidentally discharged and firing it straight into his face.

"Of course," he murmured, "we could moderate the aroma by just removing the robe..." His hands slid down the front of the soft satin and hooked into the neckline, his fingertips barely brushing the bare skin where the swell of her breasts began. She tried to control her breathing, but even inhaling in order to protest pressed her skin against his hands.

"My mother is here," Morganna pointed out.

"I forgot." Sloan didn't sound in the least repentant, and he didn't move. "Sorry, Abigail."

Abigail got to her feet. "Now that you're here, Sloan, I'm sure Morganna will excuse me."

As soon as the door closed behind her mother, Morganna shifted around on her dressing-table bench. "I assume there's a reason you popped in."

"Joel's been drifting in and out of consciousness all evening."

"Is that supposed to be good news?"

"It's better than this morning, when he was still out of it entirely. Maybe by tomorrow he'll be able to tell us why he went into my office, and exactly what happened."

"I thought the nurse said he won't be able to talk for a while."

"Not as long as he's on the ventilator, no. But there must be some way he can communicate enough to answer questions. And the investigator is pretty anxious to hear what he has to say."

Even though she had turned slightly away, he was still almost carelessly massaging her shoulders, as if he'd forgotten he was doing it. Morganna couldn't stop herself from shivering. It wasn't a shudder of displeasure, as it might have been just yesterday. Her reaction was almost the opposite, in fact—she was terrified by how easily she could lean into his touch, how natural it would feel to catch his hand and draw it down over her breast, how easily she could convince herself that this was real and not merely a mechanical act on his part...

He stepped away from her without even a lingering touch.

Morganna opened her mouth to tell him that since Abigail knew their secret, they could stop pretending. The sooner she did so, she knew, the better it would be— for then she would no longer have any excuse to torment herself with fantasy. If he wasn't touching her, kissing her, smiling at her, then she couldn't pretend that all those things meant anything.

But if he wasn't touching, kissing, smiling, then everything would be exactly as it had been before Abigail came—when the only time they'd made physical contact was in public when he offered his arm and good manners said she couldn't turn him down. Kisses and smiles hadn't even been in the repertoire back then.

And if they returned to the old ways, Abigail—romantic though she was—could not avoid seeing how cold things really were between them. In the face of that reality, she couldn't possibly maintain her illusion that they were working toward harmony and that only time stood in the way of happy wedlock. And once she knew the truth, Abigail would be just as agonizingly unhappy as Morganna was.

There was no escape for Morganna from the bargain she had made. The only saving grace was that her mother still didn't realize the full price she had paid—and what possible benefit could there be in letting Abigail discover the truth?

"You were going to say something," Sloan prompted.

Morganna knew she should tell him that their charade had not been effective after all. But events once set in motion couldn't be stopped. Words once spoken could never be silenced. Once she confessed that Abigail was onto them, there would be no taking the news back. And if that decision ultimately led to Abigail being miserable...

I'll think it over tonight. I can still tell him tomorrow. Surely there was no harm in a small delay. It wasn't as if she intended to lie, she just needed time to consider the best way to present the truth so no one—particularly Abigail—would be harmed.

Simply delaying the decision made Morganna feel insanely comforted, and the relief spilled into her voice. "It was nothing. A question about Joel, I think. I don't even remember what it was, now."

He said nothing more except good-night. Morganna was still sitting at her dressing table when he went out, and she stayed there a long time more, while moonlight made trails across the carpet and questions chased themselves through her mind.

In the morning, Selby brought Morganna her breakfast tray and the news that her mother had torn into a dress box, which he said was the size of a compact car, the moment it had been delivered. "As if it were Christmas morning, Miss Morganna," he said, sounding scandalized at the idea of Abigail Ashworth making such a first-class mess in the public areas of the house. "Then she remembered a breakfast appointment and simply left the box sitting in the middle of the hall."

"I know, Selby," Morganna sympathized. "She's changed since she moved to Phoenix, hasn't she? It's like her second childhood or something." Despite her soothing tone, however, she was a bit concerned herself. This kind of behavior didn't sound like Abigail.

By the time Morganna got downstairs, white tissue paper was strewn all over the hall carpet, and the beaded bodice of the gown she was to wear at the Carousel Ball peeked out over the top of the box. Abigail was nowhere to be seen.

Morganna could understand the temptation her mother had felt—in fact, she couldn't resist it herself. She was pulling out yet another layer of tissue from the folds of fuchsia taffeta when the doorbell rang, and since she was closest she went to answer it.

The fire investigator stepped over the threshold. "Is Mr. Montgomery at home?"

"I don't know," Morganna said. "I'll have to check." Selby came from the back of the house and she asked, "Do you know where Mr. Montgomery is?"

"In his library, ma'am. I'll tell him that the investigator is here, but I believe he's on the telephone, and he said earlier that he might be unavailable for some time.''

''There you have it,'' Morganna told the investigator. ''Straight from the expert. Thanks, Selby.''

Selby knocked and went into the library.

The investigator showed no sign of leaving. ''The butler keeps better track of your husband's whereabouts than you do.'' There was a note of disbelief in his voice.

Morganna had had her limit. ''Yes,'' she said sweetly. ''But then, you see, it's his job—not mine.'' She turned back to the dress box.

''We found the point of origin of the fire,'' the investigator said. ''And the cause.''

She frowned. ''Does that mean you can make an arrest?''

''Not yet. But we're closer, now that we know exactly where the fire started. It was on your husband's desk. There were flash burns all around the base of the desk lamp. And the lightbulb was broken—of course, that wasn't unusual, because of the heat in that room. But when I found some of the pieces, it turns out there was gasoline on the glass.''

Morganna shrugged. ''I thought you said there was nothing in that office which wasn't soaked in gasoline.''

''Oh, no, there wasn't all that much, just enough to really set off the natural gas. What's significant about the lightbulb is that the gasoline was inside it.''

''*Inside*... But it couldn't be. Lightbulbs are sealed.''

''Oh, it's possible to take one apart. Our arsonist used great care to dismantle the bulb, fill it with gasoline and glue it back together. Then he reinserted it into the lamp. When your guy in the hospital turned it on, the filament sparked, the vapor blew, and wham—a flash fire creating that very nice even burn pattern on top of the desk and setting off the cloud of natural gas." He added dispassionately, "If he hadn't been standing off to one side when it went, he wouldn't have a face left."

Morganna shuddered. *If it had been Sloan...* "I'm sure Joel will find that a great comfort."

He didn't seem to hear the sarcasm in her voice. "Mrs. Montgomery, you wouldn't happen to know if that lamp was hooked up to the wall switch or if it had to be turned on separately?"

"I don't know any of the details about my husband's business."

The investigator's eyes rested thoughtfully on the crystal beads that rimmed the neckline of the ball gown lying at her feet. "I'd already gathered that you're mainly interested in the money it brings in."

Morganna bit her tongue hard.

Selby came out of the library, and a moment later Sloan appeared in the doorway to greet the investigator. "Come in. What can I do for you?"

He didn't invite Morganna to join them, to her relief. She started gathering up tissue paper so she could repack the ball gown enough to carry it upstairs.

Though the house was solid and almost soundproof, the investigator hadn't quite closed the door behind him, so over the slight rustle of tissue Morganna could hear the two men's voices.

"The employees you terminated the morning of the fire," the investigator said. "It appears they've got a string of witnesses as to where they were all evening."

Her hands stilled on the fuchsia taffeta. How could that be?

"But Joel saw them there," Sloan protested. "One of them, at any rate."

"I didn't say they had unbreakable alibis. There could

be gaps. And I didn't say I wasn't going to keep looking into it.''

"Good. Because until that's settled, the insurance company is obviously not going to be cooperative about paying out so much as a cent.''

"Going broke, are you?''

The investigator sounded rather cheery about the possibility, Morganna thought.

Sloan's voice was cool. ''I'm overextended at the moment. Show me someone who wouldn't be, under the circumstances.''

"I understand that was a pretty sizable policy you were carrying. It must come as a blow to see it held up. I'll see what I can do to speed things along, sir.''

Morganna was standing in the hallway, the ball gown still cascading out of the box at her feet, when Sloan closed the front door behind the investigator. ''Is that your new dress?'' he asked. ''It's pretty. I'm going out— I've got an appointment with some real estate people to look at a couple of buildings.''

She was puzzled. ''Are you looking for another site for the factory?''

"No. Just an office space I can rent for a while, till I decide where we're going from here.''

"Then you don't know if you're going to renovate or start over?''

"Not yet. But in the meantime, I need a place to hook up some telephones and get mail delivery. That way the employees I've had to lay off will know where to come for straight information, and then we can start calling all our customers and trying to put things back together.''

"It really is a mess, isn't it?''

"In some ways, it's even worse than I expected. It's hard to tell what records we might be missing because the daily computer backups have so much duplication that it's going to take a week just to sort them all out. Just tracking down who had orders underway, who can wait for delivery till we're up and running again, and how we're going to satisfy the others, will take a while.''

Morganna said softly, "This is the kind of problem that makes you really miss Joel, I suppose."

"Yeah. He's a whiz at this sort of stuff." Sloan smiled ruefully. "He'd have had us in temporary quarters with the computers running and every one of our customers notified of the new address before the fire was even extinguished. See you later."

She stepped between him and the door. "Sloan, I heard you tell the investigator that you're financially overextended just now."

"I wish you hadn't heard that."

"I wasn't listening on purpose."

"I know you weren't. But I didn't want to worry you with it."

"If we're in financial trouble—"

"We're not. I'll grant you that right now cash is going out in a torrent, and there's nothing much coming in. I've got workers to take care of, another office to set up, money to refund to customers who paid in advance for furniture that we can't build till who knows when—"

"My father's debts still hanging over your head," she said flatly.

"Don't worry about it, Morganna. It's just business. We're not broke."

"I don't want to make it worse." She looked around, helplessly, and seized on the first item she saw. "I can send the dress back, Sloan. I don't need it."

He looked from the heap of fuchsia taffeta to her face, and smiled. "Yes, you do, sweetheart. How could one of the former queens of the Carousel Ball possibly show up for the big event in a dress she's worn before? Not only would what's-her-name Pendergast be horrified, but I'd come off looking like Scrooge.''

He kissed her cheek and was gone, leaving Morganna standing in the center of the hallway. Just one more confirmation—as if she'd needed another—that the only thing that mattered to Sloan was how things looked.

She felt like kicking the dress box all the way back to the store.

The office space Sloan rented was both small and spartan, but all he really needed was a place to spread out his paperwork and room for a half-dozen customer-service representatives to man the phones, reassuring clients as word of the fire damage continued to spread.

The thing that really annoyed him was having to pay good money to rent enough tables and chairs to furnish the place. The very idea of Sticks & Stones having to use a competitor's product would have been enough to set his teeth on edge, even if the president of Furnishings Unlimited hadn't tracked down Sloan's cell phone number and offered, in a suspiciously solicitous tone, to loan him whatever he needed.

Sloan declined just as politely, but he swore as he dropped the cell phone back in his pocket. ''If I'd been stupid enough to say yes, he'd probably have put us in a national ad campaign. 'When Sticks & Stones needs desks and chairs, it turns to Furnishings Unlimited'—or some nonsense like that.''

Across the room, Jack Hamilton, who was using a radiator in lieu of a chair, shifted uncomfortably. ''It's too bad that proposal you sent me about putting your merchandise in Tyler-Royale stores went astray. If we'd put through that deal, we'd would have warehouses full of Sticks & Stones merchandise that we could sell back to you.'' He grinned. ''At retail prices, of course.''

Sloan shook his head. ''It's probably just as well that package got hung up in the mail and went to Omaha instead of directly to you. Even if the head office had jumped on the proposal, we wouldn't have had time to build up an inventory yet.''

And that, he thought grimly, was yet another big job that would be long gone into the mists by the time he had a factory back on line. It was just one item on a list that would get longer with every day the insurance company delayed.

He reached into his briefcase for an antacid tablet but came up with only an empty wrapper. For a moment he forgot where he was, and without looking he reached to open the top drawer of the sample-size bureau which had sat under the window in his old office, the spot where he had always kept a few aspirin and cough drops and vitamins. When his fingers brushed only air instead of polished wood, the pain of loss swept over him anew.

Odd, how it hit in waves instead of all at once. But then, he supposed, the reality of everything he had lost was simply too huge to absorb in one blow, so from time to time he recalled another thing that was gone forever. And the half-dozen pieces of sample furniture, left from his predecessor's day, which had sat in a neat line under the window were certainly gone. They had probably exploded in the same blast that had blown Joel out of the office.

Strange, though, that there hadn't even been any recognizable scraps of the small-scale bureau or chair or sideboard, because his desk—though it was badly damaged—had been left standing precisely in its regular spot.

Of course it was larger and heavier, but it had also been closer to the blast.

Jack slid off the radiator and rubbed his tailbone. "Give me a list of what furniture you want and I'll see what I can find in our stores. We'll even make you a deal on the rental fees."

Sloan grinned. "You're a pal, Jack. I knew I could count on you."

"And that's why you invited me over," Jack agreed. "I'll call you at home tonight."

With nothing else he could do at the new office, Sloan picked up his briefcase and headed for home. Dusk had set in early, and Pemberton Place was already aglow. Lights spilled from the Tudor Revival house next door to the Georgian mansion, and cars were starting to line up in the street, waiting to pull into the driveway. The publisher of the Lakemont *Chronicle* was hosting a cocktail party, Sloan deduced. He waited patiently till the traffic cleared enough to let him pull into his own driveway.

A shadowy figure standing under an oak tree between the houses caught Sloan's attention, and instant suspicion flooded over him. Was this the sort of thing that Joel had seen? There must have been some odd activity around the place that had drawn him into the factory that night.

But a moment later the figure moved off toward the Tudor house and climbed the steps to the front door, and Sloan relaxed. Probably just a guest having a cigarette before going inside, he told himself.

He let himself into the house. No one was in sight, but the door of Morganna's miniature room was half-open. He wondered if he was being foolish to interpret that as a kind of invitation. Maybe, after he put his briefcase away, he'd go visit and see what happened.

He stopped dead on the threshold of his library when

he saw his desk blotter heaped with boxes. Flat velvet cases, small square containers, plain white cartons, cubical boxes. All sizes and shapes, they were piled into an irregular pyramid. And he had seen each one of them before. Though he hadn't actually kept a count, he'd bet the fire insurance check that every last piece of jewelry he'd ever given her was somewhere in that stack.

"Morganna!" he bellowed.

He heard the scrape of her stool against the hardwood floor, so he knew she'd heard the order in his voice. But she took her own sweet time to appear in the hall. "If you want to talk to me," she said sweetly, "you might try asking instead of summoning next time."

He was not about to apologize. "What the hell is this stuff doing on my desk?"

She looked past him toward the pile of boxes, as if, he thought irritably, she didn't remember what he was talking about. "I don't need diamonds and sapphires and emeralds and pearls," she said quietly. "And apparently, right now you do need money. So since I've never thought of these things as mine, I'm returning them to you."

"I don't need money badly enough to hock your jewelry."

"Hock?" She looked thoughtful. "I hadn't considered pawnshops, exactly. I brought it all to you because I thought you'd remember which jeweler each item came from so it could simply be returned."

"It's not that easy, Morganna. Jewelry doesn't come with a money-back guarantee."

"Of course. I hadn't thought of that. Well, if it comes to hocking it, I suppose I could do just as well as you could, and I'm much less busy. In fact, there's nothing else on my calendar for tomorrow."

Annoyed as he was, he had to admire how neatly she had gone around him. "You can't go from pawnshop to pawnshop with all this in tow."

Morganna considered. "Well, not alone, certainly. But Emily Hamilton might look at it as an adventure."

He stared at her for a long moment, eyes narrowed. She didn't blink.

"You'd probably both end up in jail on suspicion of fencing stolen property," he growled, "and Jack and I would have to come and bail you out. All right—you win. Leave the boxes where they are." Obviously, he told himself, he'd better hang onto the jewelry, if only to protect her from her own crazy impulses.

She didn't relent. "And you'll use it to make things easier on you?"

"Every last chip of it." It wasn't exactly a lie; he'd be much more relaxed if he knew that she wasn't out trolling pawnshops. "Are you happy now?"

"You're welcome, Sloan," she said quietly and turned away. The door of the miniature room closed behind her with a click.

He felt like a heel. She'd made a grand gesture—a selfless sacrifice—and he'd greeted it with anger at her and suspicion of her motives.

He sat down at his desk and opened the top box, the one shaped like a firecracker that had been her Fourth of July gift—a two-carat sapphire set in a gold star, hung on a long rope chain. He set it aside and picked up a small white velvet box which held the engagement ring he'd given her—a four-carat marquise diamond, deceptively simple and insanely expensive.

He sat with the box cupped in his hand, staring at the cold fire that lay within the stone.

Of course, he had good reason for suspecting her motives. Never in the entire six months of their marriage had one of his gifts been greeted with genuine pleasure or joy. Instead her reaction had usually been something more like resignation.

Morganna had made a grand gesture, yes, but not a selfless sacrifice. Instead, he suspected, she had felt nothing but relief when she handed his gifts back to him. She'd been pleased to have the excuse to get rid of them.

She had rejected his gifts, just as she would like to reject Sloan himself.

CHAPTER SEVEN

It HAD taken her the better part of half an hour to study all the different sorts of artists' clays on display in the university bookstore, but Morganna had finally made her decision and was lifting the largest available carton from the bottom shelf when Emily Hamilton came around a corner and almost bumped into her.

"I thought I heard you over here talking to a sales-clerk," Emily said. She eyed the carton in Morganna's arms. "That's a lot of clay. Are you going to start throwing pots?"

Morganna shook her head. "It's the wrong kind to use on a potter's wheel. There's a special clay for everything these days—or at least the store is carrying more varieties than when I was in art school. What are you doing hanging out at the campus bookstore?"

"Taking an advance look at the textbooks for a few classes I'm considering signing up for."

"You're going back to school? But you have a degree, and it's even in a field that will let you earn a living."

"A very boring living. And I was in such a hurry to get through school that I never deviated from the classes that were required for my major. So now I'm going to start taking the interesting things I missed back then. I was thinking of linguistics, maybe, or a class called The Politics of Waste Recycling, but—"

"I wouldn't call either of those an amusing little hobby," Morganna mused.

"Judging by the reading lists the professors have

116

posted," Emily said, "I'll have to agree with you. I was also thinking of art appreciation, even though the textbook needs to be outfitted with its own set of wheels. Hey, why don't you come and take something with me? Not art appreciation, of course, because you'd make the rest of us look bad. But we could both sign up for the seminar about who really wrote Shakespeare."

"I don't think so, Emily."

Emily gave a little sigh. "I know Sloan doesn't like the idea of you working, but he surely couldn't object to you taking a class one night a week."

Right now he might, Morganna thought. Nicolet University was one of the ten most ruinously expensive institutes of higher education in the nation. A single class there could cost as much as an entire semester at another university. And when the class was only for entertainment's sake, the fact that the university was also one of the ten best in the country didn't help to justify the cost.

She wondered exactly what Sloan had meant when he'd said he was overextended. Could she believe his reassurance, or was he simply trying to keep her from finding out how bad things really were?

In her own way, Morganna realized, she'd been just as foolishly trusting as her mother had been in leaving money matters entirely to the man of the family. Of course, the situations were a little different—there'd never been any question of her marriage to Sloan being a true partnership. Trophy wives didn't ask questions; it was one of the rules.

Emily obviously interpreted her failure to answer as a refusal. "How long are you going to let Sloan keep you shut up in that house, Morganna?"

Her innate sense of fairness made Morganna protest. "He doesn't do anything of the sort."

"Right." Emily's voice dripped sarcasm. "He lets you go out to play bridge, to go shopping, or to make a good impression for him at events like the Carousel Ball. Otherwise he expects you to be right there waiting for him like a proper little Victorian wife."

"What's the matter, Emily? It's not like you to snipe at Sloan. He hasn't shut me off from my friends, and you know it. He's never tried."

"Well, whoever set up the rules, you've certainly paid the price."

Morganna took a deep breath. Saying it aloud wasn't going to be easy, but it was important that she not run away from the truth Abigail had forced her to face. "The fact is I've kept myself isolated, because it's been easier to hide and luxuriate in self-pity than it has been to face everyone and pretend to be happy."

"You can't live like this forever, Morganna. When are you going to put a stop to it?" Emily sighed. "Not that I expect to get an answer. Come on, let's get out of here before the weight of that block of clay stretches your arms clear to the floor. I'll buy you a hot-fudge sundae."

She waited nearby while Morganna paid her bill, and they walked down the row of shops to the avant-garde ice-cream parlor. The lunch rush was over and only a few patrons remained, but most of the antique twisted-iron tables in the center of the room were still covered with used dishes. Emily headed for the most isolated booth in the shop, one of the few that had already been cleared.

Morganna ordered a cappuccino instead of ice cream, and she cradled the cup in her hand while she thought about what Emily had said. *When are you going to put a stop to it?* Emily had been talking about Sloan and their marriage, but even Emily didn't know all the details.

She didn't know how impossible it was for Morganna to call a halt.

But her question was still just as valid. When was Morganna going to stop hiding and wallowing in self-pity? To stop burying herself in her miniatures and rejoin the world?

Morganna eyed the shopping bag which she'd set on the seat beside her handbag. The block of clay it held represented a new twist for her, that was true—but it was a direction that wasn't actually so very much different from her other pastimes. This would be just one more project that would allow her to keep to herself instead of being with other people.

Maybe, she thought, as soon as she'd finished her coffee, she should return it to the store and get her money back, and do something very different instead.

The circumstances of her life weren't going to alter anytime soon. But Morganna could approach those circumstances from a whole new angle...if she chose.

She looked around, and the waitress, clearing a nearby table of dishes and the scattered sections of a newspaper, said promptly, "Is there something else you'd like, ma'am?"

"No," Morganna said. "Unless—is that today's *Chronicle?* If someone left it behind—"

"You're welcome to it. I was just going to throw it away." The waitress handed it over.

Emily sat up straight. "You mean you haven't already read the paper today?"

Something in the tone of her voice warned Morganna. "No. Why?" Without waiting for an answer, she shook out the newspaper and instead of turning to the classifieds to check the job listings as she'd intended to do, she looked at the front page.

A headline stretching all the way across the page announced, Investigation Continues In Sticks & Stones Fire. Under it was a photograph of the burned factory building and a complete reprise of the fire and the investigation. She read the story slowly and folded the paper with shaking hands. "This reads as if the reporter set out to make Sloan look like a liar."

Emily didn't look at her. "It doesn't say anything which—strictly speaking—isn't true."

"Surely you don't believe all these implications, Emily!" She picked up the paper again and read, "'Sticks & Stones owner Sloan Montgomery told investigators that company controller Joel Evans summoned him to the factory, saying that he'd seen someone running from the building. Investigators have been unable to confirm the presence of any such individual—' The reporter might as well have come straight out and said he thinks Sloan made it all up!"

"Because they haven't found the guy yet doesn't mean he wasn't there," Emily agreed. "And no, I don't believe everything I read in the newspaper. But it isn't just the story that looks so bad, Morganna, it's the circumstances."

Morganna said warily, "What are you talking about?"

Emily bit her lip, and when she finally spoke she sounded reluctant. "The fire investigator came to talk to Jack and me."

"Why?"

"Because we were with you that night for dinner. He asked if we could confirm what Joel told Sloan, or what Sloan said to Joel. Or even whether it was really Joel who made the call. But we couldn't swear to any of it, because we didn't hear the conversation. Remember the way Sloan stepped away from the table as soon as his phone rang?''

Morganna nodded. "But he always does that. It's simply good manners.''

"I understand that, but the fire investigator didn't seem to know anything about cell phone etiquette. And he just kept hammering questions at us—about the business, about Sloan... Jack thinks the investigator is convinced that the men Sloan terminated did not set the fire.''

"But that's impossible! Who else would have hated Sloan enough to set him up that way?''

"I don't know,'' Emily said drearily. "But Morganna—I'm awfully afraid the investigator thinks it might have been you.''

It took Morganna more than an hour to track down the fire investigator, but she finally found him in Sloan's new office. *You might as well face them both at once,* she told herself. She bypassed Sloan's secretary without a word— she'd make an apology to the woman later, assuming she was still walking around free—and went in.

Sloan was standing beside a folding table; the investigator had turned a couple of cartons of paper into a makeshift chair and was leaning back, apparently at ease.

Sloan frowned when she came in unannounced. "Morganna? What's wrong?''

"I've just discovered from my friend Emily Hamilton that the investigator here may have some mistaken ideas about me.'' Her voice was shaking despite her efforts to steady it. "And I wanted to clear up any misunderstanding just as soon as possible.''

"That's just fine with me,'' the investigator said. "What sort of misunderstanding are we talking about?''

Morganna paused, confused. Was it possible that

Emily had misinterpreted the man's questions and jumped to a conclusion that was completely unwarranted? Or was the investigator playing dumb, believing her guilty and finagling to see what Morganna would admit to and if she'd trip herself up?

"From the tone of your questions to her," Morganna said, "she believes that you might suspect me of being the cause of the fire."

"That's ridiculous," Sloan said. His tone was curt.

Relief flooded over Morganna. She hadn't anticipated that he would leap to her defense without an instant's hesitation; she'd expected him to be as stunned and speechless as she'd been.

"Is it?" The investigator stood up and paced across the room. "Of course, I'm on the outside here, and I don't pretend to understand things like society marriages. But one thing I do understand is money. And I know that when a woman is more interested in her husband's money than she is in her husband, and the husband loses out on a big deal that threatens to bring down his business—"

Morganna turned to Sloan, wide-eyed.

"The trip to San Francisco didn't go very well," he conceded. "I didn't tell you because I didn't want you to be worried about it."

Of course, he never said much about his work. And, Morganna realized belatedly, she hadn't bothered to ask about this trip when he'd come home. So why would he volunteer bad news? If she hadn't even expressed polite interest in how things had gone, he would hardly have expected her to be understanding or sympathetic....

She was seeing a side of herself that she didn't much like. Was she really so self-centered and egotistical?

"Not telling your wife what happened doesn't mean

she didn't know," the investigator mused. "I'm sure she has other sources of information. In fact, you lost a very big account."

"We didn't lose an account," Sloan countered. "We missed out on getting a new one. There's an enormous difference between not making a new sale—however large or profitable it would be—and losing a long-standing customer that we counted on as a steady source of income."

The two men were face-to-face. Both of them seemed to have forgotten that Morganna was even in the room.

The investigator pointed out, "Just a minute ago you said this deal was important enough that she'd have worried about it. Now you say it wasn't. Which is it?"

Sloan looked irritated. "She would naturally have been concerned. I was disappointed myself. But that doesn't mean the incident would have destroyed my business."

"It might have made it a little harder to come by money for the lady's toys."

"So you're saying she torched the place? That would have been a bit shortsighted. Without a product to sell or any immediate hope of being able to produce one, I'm in a whole lot worse cash position than I was before the fire."

"Only because the insurance company hasn't paid off. If they had, she could have quicklike filed for divorce and claimed half of it."

Morganna gasped.

The investigator's gaze rested on her. "It would be much easier than getting money out of the company. It takes a lot more time to convert machines and inventory to cash than it does to reduce them to ashes."

"You're getting way out of line here," Sloan said coldly.

"Speculation is my job. I think about things like motive—and money's always a good one. And opportunity—for instance, when that lightbulb was put into the desk lamp. Seems to me it could have been just about anytime. When was your wife last in your office?"

"A couple of weeks before the fire, at least. And I used the desk lamp that afternoon. Besides, the natural gas couldn't have been turned on until the last workers were out of the building, or they'd have smelled it. By that time Morganna and I were at home, getting ready to go out for dinner."

"Did you get dressed in the same room?" the investigator asked. "Was she in your sight all the time?"

"Of course not. But you can't possibly believe that she sneaked out of the house, drove across town to the warehouse district, disarmed the sprinkler system, set up the booby trap in the desk lamp, turned on the natural gas and got all the way back to Pemberton Place without anyone missing her."

"It does seem improbable, when you put it that way," the investigator conceded. "But she could have had a little help, I suppose. There's also the nature of the trap... You know, this is a very interesting kind of arson, because it doesn't seem to have been aimed only at the building. It's much more personal than that. Do you carry insurance on your life, Mr. Montgomery?"

The insinuation hit Morganna with the weight of a boulder. Her head swam with the impact, and she had to catch herself against the wall.

"Yes, I do," Sloan said evenly. "And probably—in your opinion at least—it's a large enough sum to make it worthwhile to try to eliminate me. But then you don't know my wife. I do. And I am telling you, Morganna had nothing to do with this."

"What about the man you said you saw hanging around between your house and the one next door the other day?"

"That was a guest of our neighbors."

"Did you see him actually go inside the house?"

"No, I don't think I did. But he mingled with a group of people on the steps, so he couldn't have simply walked off afterward without being noticed. If you're implying he was an accomplice, let me assure you he was certainly not hanging around waiting to see my wife about a payoff. Now can we eliminate the nonsense and figure out who really burned my building?"

"That's what I'm trying to do," the investigator said.

After he left, the office was deadly quiet.

"I appreciate you defending me," Morganna said softly.

"My pleasure." Sloan's voice was cool.

But even as her heart stopped racing with apprehension, Morganna began to wonder about his reaction. When she'd confronted the investigator, Sloan had leaped to her defense very quickly. In fact, she'd been startled by how fast he'd responded.

As if he hadn't been surprised by the accusation. As if he had wondered about it himself, before she had brought the possibility out into the open. Had his analysis of why she couldn't have been the one who planted the booby trap had been just a little too glib, as if he'd thought it all through before?

He couldn't actually believe she'd schemed against him, or surely he wouldn't have stood up for her. But had he doubted at first and had to convince himself she was innocent?

Morganna could understand, if he had. The man would have had to be more than human not to wonder if the resentment she hadn't bothered to hide had grown into hatred.

It was really too bad, she thought wearily, that the etiquette books didn't cover situations like this. Thanking him for persuading himself that she hadn't attempted to commit murder didn't seem the tactful thing to do.

Morganna went from Sloan's new office straight to the Tyler-Royale department store, which anchored the downtown shopping area, waiting beside the only set of elevators which went all the way to the top floor. When one finally arrived, Jack Hamilton got off, settling the collar of a dark trench coat into place. Morganna hadn't seen him since the night of the fire, and it was apparent within moments that he was watching her carefully, obviously concerned about how she was holding up under the strain. "I'd like a minute, Jack," she said. "But I know you're ready to go home."

"No hurry. Come up to my office." On the top floor, he led the way down a narrow hall, past the credit department and the human resources center and a long row of employee lockers.

His secretary said, "I tried to catch you, Mr. Hamilton. The package from the Omaha warehouse that you've been waiting for finally arrived. I put it on your desk."

"Thanks, Mary." He waved Morganna past the secretary's desk and on into a room that looked like a converted broom closet. Draping his trench coat over the back of a chair, he reached for the fat envelope on his desk blotter. "Excuse me for a moment," he said. "I just need to make sure this is what I was waiting for."

Morganna sat down.

"If I can even find it amongst the misdirected mail," he muttered, scattering the contents over his desk. "Now it's not only stuff from Sticks & Stones that's going astray but other things as well." He tossed a glossy catalog toward the corner of the desk.

It slid off and Morganna caught it automatically. "Furnishings Unlimited," she mused. "I wonder if Sloan has seen this."

"Take it if you like." Jack flipped through a more-subdued sheaf of papers and then dropped the packet into his briefcase. "What can I do for you, Morganna?"

"Six months ago we talked about me working for you. Designing store displays and windows. I'd like to have that job now, Jack."

His voice was gruff. "Are things that bad?"

"I don't need a paycheck so we can eat this week, no." The fact that she didn't know exactly how badly the fire was pinching Sloan's finances was none of Jack's business. Neither was the fact that Sloan had never told her anything substantial about his overall finances.

But she had to give Jack a reason for wanting a job. "I think it's time for me to start filling my days with something more productive than what I've been doing for the past six months."

"What does Sloan think about this?"

Morganna looked at him levelly. "He doesn't know about it."

Jack shifted in his chair. "If I'd known you were still interested... I'm sorry, Morganna, but I can't hire you. We just signed a contract with an outside firm to do all our design and display work. They'll be using their own employees."

"I see." She'd known, of course, that it was unlikely the job would still be open. But she'd told herself that even if Jack turned her down, it wouldn't hurt to try.

She'd been wrong. It had hurt.

"I can give you a recommendation if you want to go talk to them, but—"

"No, thanks. Not just now, anyway." She gathered up her belongings. "I appreciate your time, Jack."

It was dusk when she got to Pemberton Place, and as she came in the side door of the Georgian mansion, Sloan came out of his library. "Where have you been?"

He sounded angry, and Morganna was just tense enough herself that the tone of his voice pushed her over the edge. She set down her shopping bag with a thud and dug her fists into her hips. "This is a new twist—having to account to you for what I do with my time. I suppose next I won't be allowed to go out at all if I haven't gotten permission." Too late, she glanced past him and saw her mother standing at the bottom of the stairs.

So much for maintaining the fiction that we're even trying to get along, she thought wearily. And here she'd been feeling guilty about not telling him that Abigail had figured out their secret... She might as well have been honest, since trying to keep up the pretense was obviously doing no good at all.

"Dammit, Morganna, you can't seriously think our arsonists are likely to stroll into Pemberton Place, ring the doorbell and tell Selby they have orders to replace every lightbulb in the house. They'd be much more likely to go after a woman alone in a car. I just want you to be careful."

Abigail crossed the hall. "You're both under so much pressure," she said gently, laying one hand on Sloan's chest and the other on Morganna's shoulder. "I can feel the tension in both of you. I have an idea. Why don't we all go somewhere for a few days? Relax, get some sun—"

"Sorry, Abigail," Sloan said curtly. "I still have a

business to run. It's not the same kind of business it was last week, but it's even more important that I be here during the crisis.''

"Of course,'' Abigail said. She straightened his tie and smiled up at him.

A pang shot through Morganna at the sight of how easily the two of them interacted.

"And I know better than to ask again if Morganna will go without you.'' Abigail drifted off, looking thoughtful.

Morganna waited till her mother was out of earshot. "I'm sorry I yelled at you,'' she said stiffly.

Sloan nodded. "So am I. It's been a long day for both of us.'' He turned back toward the library. "And I have a lot to do yet.''

Morganna told herself that it was just as well that he'd walked away. What had she been about to do, anyway? Suggest they go for a stroll around the neighborhood? Invite him to join her for a drink and a tête-à-tête? Whatever she'd said, it would have come out all wrong.

She picked up the shopping bag and went into the miniature room, where she sat for a couple of minutes and stared at the circus-theme room box. Then she dug the block of clay out of the bag and tore it open.

Making miniatures might be a dangerously solitary pastime, she thought. Perhaps even a compulsive one. But at least the tiny inanimate objects didn't talk, or demand anything from her. And right now, that kind of peace and quiet was exactly what she needed.

The bridge game was almost over when Morganna realized what had been bothering her all afternoon about Emily. Not only had she been practically silent, but she kept stealing glances at the Carousel Ball portrait of

Morganna that hung above the drawing-room mantel.
What was that all about? she wondered.

Sherrie gathered up the cards and began to shuffle. "I
don't suppose we have time to play another."

Morganna looked automatically at her wrist, forgetting
for a moment that she'd given the platinum watch back
to Sloan along with the rest of her jewelry. "I don't even
know what time it is."

"After three o'clock," Emily said. She pushed her
chair back.

Sherrie put the cards down. "What happened to your
watch, Morganna?"

"I'm just not wearing it today." The evasion felt like
a lie.

"And you forgot your engagement ring, too, I see,"
Sherrie murmured.

From across the table Carol said, "If I owned a rock
like that one, I'd never forget to put it on."

"You did just forget it—right?" Sherrie said.
"Because the rumor that's flying around town says that
every jewel you used to own is in a bank vault somewhere as security for a loan to keep Sloan afloat for a
week or two longer."

Emily said sharply, "That's ridiculous."

Morganna was relieved not to have to answer. What
could she have said, anyway—that she didn't know
where her jewelry was or exactly how Sloan was putting
it to use?

She saw Sherrie and Carol out and closed the front
door behind them with relief. "No question, I have got
to find something better to do with my time than bridge,"
she muttered. "Can you stay a minute, Emily? I have
something I want to show you." She led Emily into the

miniature room, where the circus-theme room box sat alone on a display pedestal.

Emily's eyes widened. She carefully stepped closer.

Morganna tried to look at the room box as if she, like Emily, had never seen it before. The lion-cage bed, the popcorn-cart desk, the circus train which perched on its room-encircling track. But what she was really interested in was Emily's reaction to the sculpted clay figure of a little boy, less than four inches long, who sprawled across the carpet looking at a comic book. He was complete with freckles, a scrape on his elbow, and mud encrusted on his infinitesimal running shoes.

Morganna reached around to the back of the room box and flipped a hidden switch. The train started to chug around the room, and the tiny carousel began to revolve and play carnival music.

But Emily was still looking at the doll. "So that's why you were buying special clay. You've never done dolls before, so what made you decide to add one this time?"

Morganna shrugged. "Something Sloan said, I guess—about the scenes being chilly without people. I thought it was worth a try. I think I'll give him a playmate, too. And maybe a dog. What do you think?"

"Do you have time? The ball's only a couple of days off." Emily didn't wait for an answer. "About Sloan... I saw Millicent Pendergast at the country club today, Morganna. She told me she's withdrawing Sloan's invitation to host the Carousel Ball."

"But she can't do that," Morganna protested.

"You know Millicent does whatever she wants where the Carousel Ball is concerned. She thinks she owns it. Her excuse is that she isn't actually disinviting him, because he never formally agreed to be a host."

"It was the night of the fire that she asked him. He's had a few other things on his mind since then."

"I mentioned that. I even suggested that she call him and ask. She said very virtuously that rather than bother him when he's so busy, she's just going to consider that he refused the honor."

"Well, we'll see what she says to me when I point out that if she'd invited him on time in the first place, instead of delaying for as long as humanly possible, she'd have had an answer long before the fire."

"Morganna, you might not want to push it. Why do you think she told me what she was going to do?"

"Because she knew you'd pass it on to me, of course."

"I don't suppose she was doing it out of fondness for you, but she has handed you a good excuse not to show up at the ball. Sloan *is* busy, and—"

"Why wouldn't we... You mean we might want to hide our heads because of that rumor Sherrie mentioned this afternoon?"

"It's not the only one, honey. I've heard half a dozen more at least, and they're even uglier. I have to get home. But I wanted you to be warned about Millicent and have a chance to think about what you're going to do." Her gaze rested on the room box. "And I want that, too. I wonder how much I'll have to pay at the auction."

"Good question," Morganna mused. "Just don't hold your breath about it being there, if Sloan isn't welcome."

As if her mention of his name had summoned him, Sloan was coming up the steps to the side door as Emily left. He looked tired, Morganna thought, and she wasted a moment wishing that she was on the same easy terms with him that her mother was. Abigail would probably have taken one look at him and ordered him to sit down so she could rub his neck.

Instead Morganna moved back from the door so he didn't have to brush past her. "What's happened?"

"They took Joel off the ventilator today."

But that should be good news, she thought. "Does that mean he can talk?"

"He's got a pretty sore throat from the tubes—but yes. He can talk."

"So it's all right now."

"Not exactly. He told the investigator he doesn't remember going into the building or walking into my office, much less turning on the lamp."

"Shock, I suppose," Morganna said. "It must have been so painful that his mind just blotted out the explosion. But surely he confirmed that he saw a man running away before he went inside?"

Sloan shook his head. "He doesn't remember anything after he pulled up in front of the building. And the doctors say, considering the odd ways that amnesia works, he may never remember."

And that meant he couldn't confirm what he had told Sloan that night. "Now what?"

"I don't know. The good news is that it appears you're off the hook with the investigator, Morganna."

She frowned. "He doesn't suspect me anymore? How did that happen?"

Sloan's smile held no humor. "Because now he seems to think I did it myself."

CHAPTER EIGHT

MORGANNA said flatly, "That's absolute nonsense. Burn your own building? Destroy your own business? Why?"

"He doesn't seem to have settled on a precise motive. But the usual one is that the owner no longer wants to be involved in the business. Either it's losing money, or he wants to sell but there's no interested buyer, or he just wants to get cash as quickly as possible and collecting on insurance appears to be the fastest way."

"Anyone who wanted a quick payoff from an insurance company would surely put a little more thought into making the fire look accidental," Morganna mused. "And anyway, those things aren't true with Sticks & Stones."

Sloan shook his head. "No, but I suppose that's why the investigator is still looking. His parting shot when we left the hospital was something about all the long-standing customers I've lost lately. I pointed out that he hasn't seen anything yet—because I'm out of business for the foreseeable future, I'm bound to lose a whole lot more. The CEO of Furnishings Unlimited must be drooling about now. All he has to do is figure out who's been buying from Sticks & Stones and move in on them while I'm dead in the water."

"And the investigator thinks you did this on purpose? Maybe he needs to find a new job. Like teaching people how to write adventure stories—he seems to have a knack for constructing far-fetched plots. What kind of idiot does he think you are, anyway?"

Sloan started to laugh.

Morganna wrinkled her nose. "I meant that as a compliment."

"I know you did. That's why it was so funny." The back of his hand brushed casually against her hair.

Morganna held her breath for an instant, but he didn't follow up. "I was trying to say that if you'd been arranging a fire, the cause wouldn't have been apparent."

"Oh, he's giving me credit for realizing how difficult it is to hide arson completely," Sloan said wryly. "He seems to think I might have set an obvious fire, thinking that no one would seriously believe I could be that stupid."

"But why would you have set up a trap in your own office? Why not just settle for burning the building?"

"Perhaps because I was trying to throw suspicion on someone else by making myself look like a target."

Morganna shook her head in disbelief. "By arranging a blast that could only be set off by turning on a desk lamp?"

"Touching any metal part of the lamp would have been enough to complete the circuit and turn on the bulb, actually."

"It doesn't matter exactly how it was triggered. My point is, whoever set it off had to be within an arm's length of the lamp. If you were going to arrange what looked like a hit on yourself, wouldn't you have figured out a way to touch it off without getting hurt?"

"I think he believes anyone who would set up that kind of a trap in the first place wouldn't care who happened to get in the way. Besides, someone would be bound to go snooping on the boss's desk sooner or later. Or I suppose I could have sent my secretary in to get something for me."

Morganna shivered. She couldn't even imagine someone who was inhuman enough to deliberately cause to any person the sort of injuries Joel had received. To do so without caring who was hurt—without having even the feeble excuse of wanting revenge against a specific person—was more than she could comprehend.

But this entire accusation was fiction, she reminded herself. No matter how plausible a story the investigator eventually managed to construct, there was no evidence to back it up. And without proof, the scenario was no threat to Sloan.

Except, of course, for the fact that the longer the investigator pursued blind alleys, the longer it would be until there was any settlement at all—and by that time, Sticks & Stones might be too far gone to resuscitate.

And except for the fact that suspicion could be an even more destructive force than fact was.

No matter how much the investigator might want to accuse Sloan of arson, he couldn't possibly prove it—and so he was unlikely to make the charge at all. But just as the investigator couldn't prove that Sloan had set the fire, Sloan would find it impossible to show conclusively that he hadn't.

There were already half a dozen ugly rumors flying around Lakemont, Emily had said. And the trouble with a rumor was that it was difficult to deny. It was difficult to defend against, because any attempt to explain simply drew more attention to the original story. And it was difficult to weed out of the nooks and crannies where it lurked, ready to spring up again at any time.

On Saturday morning, Sloan finished reading the *Chronicle's* newest story about the Sticks & Stones fire, folded the newspaper and laid it beside his breakfast plate, and picked up his coffee cup.

He wished he had sources as knowledgeable as those of the *Chronicle's* reporter. Then he might at least have had a warning that the two men he'd terminated on the morning of the fire had proved to have solid alibis after all. Instead he'd found it out along with the rest of Lakemont. Why hadn't the fire investigator told him?

So now what? Frustration made him unwilling to sit and wait, watching his business evaporate, while the investigation limped on. But he was damned if he knew what else he could do.

The dining-room door opened, and from the corner of his eye he watched Morganna come in. During the six months of their marriage, he could count on one hand the mornings when she'd actually come downstairs for breakfast. But of course she would have to choose the one day when he was at his lowest ebb and in no mood to play games. "Good morning," he said, and raised his cup to his lips.

She took one look at him and said, "Let me have the newspaper."

He handed it to her. "I don't know why you'd think there's something in it worth reading."

"The fact that you haven't noticed your coffee cup is empty is a dead giveaway that you have something new and important on your mind." She opened the *Chronicle* with a snap and went straight to the story.

Sloan refilled his cup and watched her face tighten as she read it.

She hadn't bothered to get dressed this morning, he noted. She wasn't wearing any slinky purply-pink dressing gown today, though. She was wrapped from throat to toes in basic blue terry cloth. She probably thought it was just as nonrevealing as a nun's habit.

And, to be fair, Sloan thought, it probably would be—to someone who had never seen her wearing the sexy purply-pink thing. Or a backless gown, a silky sweater, a short skirt, or a low-necked dinner dress—all of which, on Morganna, looked equally sexy. But Sloan had spent six months collecting views of Morganna and assembling them in his mind, and a thick blue terry-cloth robe wasn't enough to block his mental vision.

To be perfectly truthful, he admitted, the nun's habit wouldn't have slowed him down much, either.

Morganna put the paper down with a slap. "Then who did Joel see running from the building?"

"You've gone straight to the heart of the problem. I don't know."

She frowned. "Who could it have been? Who could he possibly have mistaken for those men? Didn't you say there was a homeless man living in the empty lot across the street?"

"He was there last summer. Now that it's colder I'm sure he's moved on."

"That's the answer," Morganna said triumphantly. "He broke into the building to try to keep warm. Maybe he was trying to start up the heater in your office when—"

"With a lightbulb full of gasoline?"

"That is a problem," she admitted. She propped her elbows on the table and put her chin in her hands. Then she frowned and looked around the room. "Hasn't Mother come down yet? Her bedroom door was open."

"She's been and gone. She asked if she could borrow your car. I told her she could take the Jag but she said she'd rather drive yours. I hope you don't mind."

"That you gave her permission?" Morganna shook her head. "It's your car more than mine anyway. I'm not the one who bought it."

Her tone was perfectly casual. She hadn't even stopped to think about what she was saying, he realized. She obviously wasn't trying to start an argument. She wasn't even accusing him of acting overbearing by not consulting her wishes. As far as she was concerned, she was simply stating a fact.

She'd have no doubt given the car back to him along with all of her jewelry, if she'd thought of it.

"Oh, I know where she is," Morganna said. "She took her tiara to the jewelers."

"Tiara?" Sloan asked doubtfully.

"There were a couple of stones loose when she got it out of the attic yesterday, so she had to rush it in for a repair before tonight," Morganna said. He must have looked blank, for she added impatiently, "The Carousel Ball—remember?"

He'd forgotten all about it, Sloan realized. "It's almost funny, in a painful sort of way—how things that used to seem so important suddenly lose all their meaning."

Morganna tensed till she was almost rigid. "You're not thinking of backing out, are you, Sloan?"

She looked as if it would be the end of her world if he did. And it was true that Lakemont society would certainly notice—and comment upon—a former queen of the ball who was stranded at the last minute without an escort because her husband had a thousand more important things to do than cater to her social pretensions.

But what did it matter to him what they said? His main reason for caring what society thought of him was that he wanted his children to someday have things easier than he had. But since Morganna had made it clear that the possibility of them ever having children was so slender it was invisible, he had no reason to put himself to any great effort on her behalf.

He opened his mouth to tell her he wasn't going. It was only a dance, after all. Let someone else step in and fill his shoes, someone who might actually enjoy spending a good part of the evening making hypocritical small talk with girls who were barely out of their teens.

When he saw Morganna's eyes, however, dark and wide in a face white with anxiety, he couldn't say it. On the other hand, he was damned if he'd admit that a wistfully pleading look had been enough to bring him to heel.

"Back out," he said dryly, "and have to face your mother's wrath? Not a chance."

At the nurses' station, Morganna learned that Joel had been moved from the trauma unit into a private room. She felt relieved by the news until she found the room and realized how much high-tech equipment still surrounded him, humming and clicking and beeping in a soft, almost syncopated rhythm. He was still obviously a very sick man.

He was asleep when she came in, and she tiptoed to the chair which stood beside his bed, and quietly sat down to wait. She'd stay for a few minutes, she decided, but if he hadn't awakened by then she'd leave a note along with the flowers she'd brought and visit again another day.

He lay flat on his back. One leg was in a cast, his foot suspended from a bar above the bed. His head was tipped back and turned slightly away from the door so that from her chair Morganna saw him only in profile. The part of his face that she could see looked a bit swollen, but otherwise he appeared amazingly normal, considering what he'd been through. Far better than he had the night of the fire, she thought. The damage must have been much less extensive than it had looked on the first night.

Then she looked at his hands and wanted to cry. Splints and gauze bandages held each finger separate, and on one palm she could see shiny, deep red patches.

He stirred restlessly. "Who's there?" he said gruffly. "Come around so I can see you."

Of course, she thought. With his hands so restricted, he couldn't easily move himself. She walked around the bed. "It's Morganna, Joel. Sloan told me you were better and could have company now."

She got her first good look at the rest of his face, and it took every bit of self-control she possessed not to show the shock she felt. He hadn't escaped lightly after all; at the moment of the explosion, he'd simply had his head turned in such a way that one side of his face had taken the brunt of the blast. That half was badly swollen, angry red, and blistered. Patches of his hair had been singed, and one eyebrow had completely disappeared, leaving him looking quizzical.

"So you came to look at the monster."

Morganna hardly recognized his voice; it was gruff and raspy—no doubt the lingering effects of the ventilator tubes. "No. I came to visit a friend."

"Right." Sarcasm dripped from the word. "So Sloan told you I was better, did he? Easy for him to say. He's not lying here in splints and casts and bandages, not even able to move to a more comfortable position."

She leaned on the bed rail. "You must be very angry and resentful right now."

He laughed bitterly. "Don't bother trying to sound understanding, Morganna. I've had just about as much sympathy as I can take from people who don't have a clue what they're talking about, because they've never looked at the world from this side.''

''We'll do everything we can to get you back to normal, Joel.''

''Normal? You think I'll ever be normal again?'' He began to swear.

A voice from the doorway cut across the stream of words. ''I'd say your visit hasn't exactly been soothing, Mrs. Montgomery.'' The fire investigator came to the opposite side of the bed.

Morganna's fingers clenched on the rail. ''I haven't been deliberately upsetting him, if that's what you think.''

''It usually doesn't take much to set off a burn victim, to remind him that he innocently made just one wrong move and now his life will never be the same.'' He tipped his head to one side and looked closely at her. ''Do you mind if I ask you a question?''

''Not at all,'' Morganna said sweetly, ''as long as you don't mind if I don't answer without consulting an attorney first.''

The investigator laughed. ''Oh, it's nothing like that. I just wanted to hear your description of your husband's office. You did visit your husband's office at one time or another, didn't you?''

''Once in a while,'' Morganna said warily. ''Why do you want my opinion?''

''The woman's point of view. Ask a man what's in a room and he'll say, 'Just the usual stuff.' No details. But women—now women notice things.''

''I hadn't been in the factory for a couple of weeks at least. So anything I remember isn't necessarily the way it was the night of the fire.''

The investigator nodded. ''I'll consider what you tell

me to be only background information. You're just helping me to visualize things.''

Morganna hesitated, but she couldn't see any reason not to answer. ''It *was* a pretty basic office. From the doorway, you looked straight across to the window over the factory floor. The desk was in between, with one end pushed up against the wall on the left side. Sloan liked to sit with his back to the window, because that way he could just stand up and see what was going on down on the production line. There were a couple of chairs between the doorway and the desk, for visitors.''

''Anything else in the office?''

Joel muttered, ''There was a row of little furniture under the window.''

Morganna was startled. He'd gone so silent that she thought he'd drifted off to sleep once more.

''Little furniture?'' the investigator asked doubtfully. ''Like what?''

''I'd forgotten about that,'' Morganna said. ''The pieces were sales samples from decades ago. It was real furniture, built the same way the full-size pieces were. But these were made small enough to haul around to show to the customer.''

The investigator looked at Joel. ''Were the pieces there the night of the fire?''

Joel didn't open his eyes. ''I can't remember any more today than I did yesterday.''

''Too bad.'' The investigator looked at Morganna. ''Anything else?''

Morganna racked her brain. ''Nothing of special value, if that's what you're looking for.''

''I'm not looking for anything in particular. Only the truth.'' The investigator turned toward the door.

"Thanks, Mrs. Montgomery. Joel, if you remember anything, have the nurses give me a call."

Morganna put out a hand. "Just a minute, please. About those alibis... You're absolutely certain they're solid?"

"Absolutely, Mrs. Montgomery." The investigator went out.

Morganna wondered if it was her imagination, or if there really had been a tinge of sympathy in his eyes.

Morganna's hands trembled as she took her tiara from its storage box and nestled it carefully into her upswept hair. The crystals lining the elegant silvery curves caught the light and sparkled as convincingly as the diamonds they imitated. She took as deep a breath as she could manage and rose, shaking out the full skirt of the fuchsia ball gown.

Abigail was already in the drawing room, wearing peach crepe and the newly repaired tiara which was a remembrance of her own reign as queen of the Carousel Ball thirty years before. But Morganna had eyes only for Sloan, standing in front of the fire, tall and lean and incredibly good-looking in his classic black tuxedo.

His gaze swept over her and then shifted for an instant to the portrait above the mantel. She wondered what differences he saw between the real woman and the painted one. Did the strain she was feeling show, despite her best efforts?

Apparently it did, for he handed her a champagne flute and said, "I know that seeing Joel this afternoon upset you, Morganna. I feel guilty every time I leave his room, because he's stuck there. But it won't do him any good for you to let it ruin your special evening."

She appreciated the sentiment, even though he was

wrong about the cause of her distress. It wouldn't be fair not to warn him, she knew—but how? She'd been trying to find the right words all the time she was dressing. "Sloan, about this evening—"

Selby announced Emily and Jack Hamilton and ushered them into the drawing room.

"It's freezing outside," Jack said.

Sloan nodded. "There's a storm hanging over the lake. It's supposed to snow by morning."

"What was Millicent thinking of to allow a little thing like weather to threaten the Carousel Ball?" Emily murmured. She accepted a glass of champagne and exclaimed over Morganna's gown. "It was a good choice not to wear a heavy necklace and bracelet with that dress, Morganna. Diamonds would have overwhelmed the effects of the tiara."

I'll have to remember that line, Morganna thought. It was as good an explanation as any for her absent jewelry.

Jack was right; the air was frigid for October. It made a handy excuse for Morganna; when the limousine dropped them off at the main entrance of Lakemont's premier hotel, she pulled her velvet cloak as close as she could and almost leaned against Sloan, not even waiting for him to offer his arm. "I need a minute with you," she whispered.

"Darling, I'm thrilled, but do you really think that right now is—"

"Dammit, Sloan, just listen to me. Millicent Pendergast has decided you're guilty, and she is counting on you not showing up tonight."

His voice was chilly. "Nice of you to warn me."

"I was afraid, if I told you before, you might decide not to come," Morganna admitted.

"Do you really think I'm a coward?" His eyes had

turned to ice. "I'm not going to run, Morganna, because I haven't done anything to be ashamed of. Or did you think I'm just too stupid to understand that I have to face down the rumors now or else I'll never overcome the suspicion?"

She was too stunned to answer, and before she found her voice Sloan had walked on toward the ballroom.

Morganna spent the half hour until the official start of the Carousel Ball constructing mental pictures of what might have gone on in the anteroom where Millicent Pendergast always gave last-minute instructions to her crew of hosts. None of the scenarios in her head were pretty. But Sloan didn't come back out—and when the lights dimmed, the orchestra struck up the first march, and the spotlights began to circle, he was part of the long parade, escorting a white-gowned debutante.

She released a long breath that she didn't know she'd been holding. "Have a little faith," Abigail said. "And smile."

Morganna applied that advice midway through the evening when, with his duty done, Sloan came looking for her, finding her standing at the edge of the dance floor talking to a man she'd known for years. To her annoyance, when she gave him her most brilliant smile, Sloan glanced over his shoulder as if to see who she'd been looking at.

"Darling," she cooed when he came up to them. She watched as wariness sprang into his eyes, and wanted to kick him. "Are you finally free? I've been standing here playing wallflower all evening, desperately regretting that I let Millicent talk me into sharing you with all the debutantes."

The man with her laughed. "Don't stretch it,

Morganna. You've turned down three invitations to dance while I've been standing here with you.''

"I hope the long, deprived evening hasn't made you forget how to waltz," Sloan said. He offered his hand. Morganna set her champagne glass aside, waved an apology to the man she'd been talking to and let Sloan draw her toward the dance floor.

"Sorry to drag you away," he said. "If you were turning down dances to stand there with him, he must be something special."

"Oh, *very* special. In fact, he was the biggest bore of my debutante year, and time hasn't improved him in the least—so I was very pleased to see you coming." That ought to put him in his place, she thought.

Sloan didn't answer.

She felt the pangs of guilt begin to gnaw; it hadn't been necessary to insult him. "If you're tired of dancing, Sloan, we could go look at the auction items."

"Oh, no. If I have to face down this crowd, so do you." He drew her a little closer. "You might try to look as if you're having a good time."

"Would you prefer me to look excited, delighted, or love-struck?"

"How about all three in turn?"

Morganna did her best. But in fact, what she couldn't help but feel was sad—for the evening could have been such a precious memory, if only they had not been pretending. To have danced the night away with the man she loved...

Well, she told herself, that was exactly what she was doing. The fact that Sloan neither knew nor cared how she felt was beside the point. So was the fact that he didn't return the feeling. She could still have a memory to treasure.

Morganna was almost sorry when late in the evening the orchestra took a break. The crowd filtered onto the mezzanine to admire the items that had been donated for the silent auction.

Automatically she sought out the room box she'd donated, and noted that it was drawing considerable attention. A small man with thick glasses was inspecting it at great length and in pinpoint detail, much to the disgust of a group standing behind him, prevented from seeing anything at all.

"I wonder if Emily paid him to block the view," Morganna murmured. "If nobody else can get a good look, she might not have to bid as high."

A wicked twinkle sprang to life in Sloan's eyes. "Emily wouldn't care. Now if you had suggested that *Jack* might have hired him to hold the price down—"

She laughed in utter relief. At least he wasn't angry with her now.

She couldn't—she *wouldn't*—ask for anything more.

The snow must have started right after they went into the ballroom, for they came outside in the small hours of the morning to an icy-cold and surreal landscape. The streets were still reasonably clear, but wet, heavy snow had piled high on trees and shrubs, bending them down till branches rested against the ground.

Jack threw himself back against the seat of the limousine and chortled.

"I can't believe you're laughing after what that room box cost you," Sloan said.

Jack waved a hand. "Oh, that's nothing. I knew the Carousel Ball would be more fun if you were there. I just didn't know how much more fun. It was great, Morganna. You'd have loved it. I thought I was going to fall down laughing when Sloan burst into that side room and kissed Millie's hand.''

Morganna's eyebrows soared. "You charmed Millicent Pendergast?"

"Actually, she was a long way from being charmed," Jack explained. "She was furious—but helpless when confronted by a perfect gentleman who insisted on acting as if he adored her."

"But I doubt she'll be inviting me next year," Sloan said. "We weren't supposed to get this much snow. And it's heavy—look at the pine trees sagging under the weight of it."

The limousine pulled into Pemberton Place and stopped in front of the Georgian mansion. "Thanks for the lift," Sloan said. "Unless you'd like to come in?"

"Oh, no," Jack said easily. "Not that we wouldn't enjoy being snowbound with you, but if the electricity's going to go out, I'd rather be at home." He gave a wicked chuckle. "With my wife, who owes me for a very expensive room box."

As soon as they were inside, Abigail said good-night. Sloan kissed her cheek and watched her climb the steps.

Morganna carefully wiped snow off her shoes and tried not to mind that the good-night gesture she received would not be as tender. "I'm going up, too," she said.

"Morganna," Sloan said softly. "We need to talk."

Feeling the weight of regret settle back on her shoulders, Morganna paused in the center of the hall, not turning to face him. "I'm sorry I didn't tell you about Millie Pendergast earlier. And I'd like to make it clear that it never crossed my mind that you might be a coward."

"I wasn't asking for an apology. I was trying to make one. I shouldn't have snapped at you." He moved closer, till she could feel his warmth. "You didn't have to do that, Morganna. You could have let me walk into the trap, and enjoyed watching me be embarrassed. Why didn't you?''

She shook her head a little. She should be glad that he didn't understand all the reasons she'd done it. ''You're my husband.''

''I wish that was really true.'' The rasp of the words sounded as if his throat hurt.

Morganna shot a startled look at him.

''Oh, it's legal,'' he said. ''I'd just like it to be more than legal. I need you, Morganna.''

Her eyes filled with tears. *Is it me you need,* she wanted to ask, *or the Carousel Ball queen?* But what was the point in asking, when he might not even understand the difference? If she tried to explain, she'd certainly give herself away. And that she could not bear.

As if he had heard the unspoken question, he whispered, ''I need you, Morganna. Just you.''

She looked up at him for what seemed forever, her gaze searching his face. Then she gave a little sigh and took a half-step toward him. Slowly and carefully, she laid her palms flat against his shoulders. ''In that case, Sloan...'' Her voice was hardly more than a breath. ''Let's make it more than legal.''

CHAPTER NINE

IT HADN'T been so difficult after all, Morganna thought with a tinge of surprise, to reach out to him. All this time she had been jealous of her mother's ease with Sloan, but when she had finally stepped across the invisible line she had drawn between them, it had been almost easy. And it felt so right, to stand within the circle of his arms and feel the beat of his heart under the palms of her hands.

I need you, he had said.

It wasn't everything Morganna wanted. But it was more than she had ever expected to hear him say, or even dared to hope for.

The man she had married hadn't needed anyone at all. He had chosen the wife he wanted and single-mindedly gone after her—but that was an entirely different thing. No matter how much he had wanted Morganna, she'd never been under any illusion that his life would have been ruined if she had turned down his offer. He would merely have moved on in his search for a trophy to the next suitable candidate.

No, he hadn't needed her then. But now...

The fire had changed him. It had burned away some of the self-assurance that he had used almost as armor to hold everyone around him at an emotional distance. The loss of his business had left him vulnerable—and it had made him far more lovable.

There had always been a basic inequality in their marriage—because he had rescued her, and therefore she owed him. Sloan had never put it in those terms, of course, for he had never been crude. But Morganna had always been painfully aware that at any time he could reject her as easily as he had selected her in the first place.

In a feeble attempt to protect her emotions, she had closed herself off just as effectively as he had. For a long while she had refused to admit that she loved him, because caring for him would only increase the imbalance.

But things had changed. More important, Sloan had changed. And if he needed her, then perhaps they could build a new kind of relationship, one with more symmetry between the partners. It wasn't the romantically loving marriage that she dreamed of, but for right now, the fact that he needed her was enough. And perhaps someday it could be more than that....

Don't get your hopes up, she told herself.

Before she could lose herself in dreams of what she'd like, Morganna went after what she could have. She let her hands slip from his shoulders to the back of his head, and drew his mouth down to hers.

His lips were gentle, asking rather than demanding, persuading rather than forcing. But under the softness she could taste a hunger in him that both delighted and frightened her.

She was delighted because the sensation was confirmation that making love to her was not the casual act she had once feared it would be for him. And she was frightened because she sensed that, unleashed, the hunger could consume them both.

Sloan held her away from him and looked down into her face. "I have wanted you for so very long, Morganna." Then he kissed her again and everything else melted out of her mind.

She hardly noticed climbing the stairs beside him. She barely remembered him helping to remove her tiara after she somehow got it tangled in her hair.

But she would never forget the wonder in her heart and the brilliance in his eyes as she gave herself up to him. Or the way he held her, afterward, as if he would never let her go.

Yes, he needed her...and that would be enough, after all.

He had not turned on the bedside lamps because the streetlights outside, reflecting off the falling snow, had filled his bedroom with a sort of dusky twilight, a soft and flattering background to their lovemaking. For a long time Morganna didn't even open her eyes, simply luxuriated in the peace of a snow-silenced world and a heart brimming with joy.

When she did look around, she was puzzled. "Why is it so dark?"

"Jack's prediction was right. The electricity went off a few minutes ago."

"Oh. I thought maybe—" She felt herself coloring.

"You were afraid that making love had caused you to go blind?" Sloan laughed. "Honey, you're supposed to see stars and fireworks, not sheer darkness."

"I did," she whispered.

He gathered her closer. "And so did I." His voice was husky.

"I wonder if practice makes the stars and fireworks brighter."

Sloan raised his head. "We could make a research project of it."

Before she could answer, there was a distinct click and the electricity came back on. The streetlights were once more magnified by a million snowflakes. The furnace fan began to whirr. The bedside lamps glowed softly golden.

Morganna frowned. "I thought those lamps were off."

"They were. The sensors get confused sometimes when the power goes out." He leaned across her to tap the base of the lamp. When both lights were off, he settled back and snuggled her once more to his side. "Now, where were we? Something about a research project..."

"Oh, yes. We're going to find out once and for all whether you snore."

"Not tonight, we're not," he murmured. "Because tonight I have better things to do than sleep."

They did sleep eventually, and Morganna woke very late to a wonderland world frosted with snow under a brilliant blue sky. Even though it was Sunday, the household was already humming when she peeked out of the master bedroom, saw that the upstairs hall was empty, and tried to duck across to her own room.

She supposed it was inevitable, given the hour, that she couldn't manage to make it all the way without running smack into her mother. Abigail paused in midstep, her mouth twisting as if she was trying very hard not to smile.

Morganna shifted from one bare foot to the other and refused to think about the picture she must present, wearing Sloan's pleated formal shirt as a substitute dressing gown and clutching a crumpled heap of fuchsia taffeta and a tiara. It was none of her mother's business, after all.

But despite her determination not to act defensive, she heard herself saying, "I was right, he doesn't own a pair of pajamas, or I'd have borrowed them instead. So if you want to get him some for Christmas—"

"Oh, no," Abigail murmured. "I hate wasting money on things that will never be used." She moved on toward the stairway. "Good morning, Selby."

Morganna ducked for her bedroom door, but she was too late. As Selby reached the top of the stairs, he blinked once as her attire—or lack of it—registered, but his voice was as level as ever. "A gentleman has called to see you, Miss Morganna. Mr. Montgomery is entertaining him in the miniature room."

That was odd, she thought. Who would be dropping by the house to see her on a snowy Sunday morning? Not a friend, or Selby would have known the name and passed it on. And why had Sloan taken this unknown into her private lair instead of the drawing room?

She dumped her ball gown unceremoniously on her bed and grabbed for a pair of jeans and an oversized ski sweater. With her hair hastily scooped up into a knot at the back of her head, she hurried downstairs and into the miniature room.

Standing beside the model of the Georgian mansion, inspecting it with painstaking attention, was the little man with the thick glasses who had been studying her room box so carefully at the auction last night. Puzzled, she looked at Sloan, who had pulled a stool away from her worktable to perch on it. His smile was a lazily intimate reminder of the night, making her feel warm and rattled all at the same time.

"Next time," she said under her breath, "wake me up earlier so I won't be caught half-dressed in the upstairs hall."

"Next time," Sloan said just as softly, "I'll help you move all your clothes and then we can both sleep as late as we want." He glanced at the little man. "I don't know what this is about. He wanted to talk to you."

The little man turned, peering at Morganna through his thick lenses. "There are no dolls in your dollhouse," he said flatly.

Now that we've established the obvious, Morganna thought, *where do we go from here?* "No," she said. "There never have been. Making human figures to add to the miniatures is a new sideline for me."

"I came because I wanted to see more of your dolls."

She was bewildered. *Does he think this is a museum?*

"I'm not making myself clear, am I?" the little man asked. "I'm interested in purchasing some of your work."

"I've never sold anything. I've just donated pieces, like to the auction last night."

"And why is that?"

"I don't mind donating my work to a good cause, and the buyer is willing to pay a high price because they're making a donation as well. So everyone wins. But I could never charge those prices."

He nodded. "To adequately compensate you for the hours you put into each piece, your prices would have to be so high that very few people could pay them. And most would not understand why something so small should be so expensive."

Morganna relaxed a little. Despite the rocky start they'd gotten off to, the man seemed to have common sense. "That's it exactly. And if people are paying a high price, they often feel that they should be able to set the rules. For me, working on commission would take all the fun out of it. For instance, if you wanted me to reproduce your grandmother's house, but I didn't feel inspired by that subject—"

He interrupted. "I do not want a miniature of my grandmother's house. In fact, I'm not interested in the room boxes, good as they are, because many people do very good scale model rooms or even houses. I'm interested in your dolls. My apologies—your miniature figures. I shouldn't have called them mere dolls, should I? I've been involved with miniatures and scale models and toys for more than thirty years, and I've never seen anything so detailed or lifelike as the two little boys you put in the room box I saw last night.''

The figures she had added as an afterthought, as a mere finishing detail, were what had so absorbed his attention?

''That's why I came, because I wanted to see more of them.''

''There aren't any more,'' Morganna said weakly.

He pointed at the block of raw clay which still stood on her worktable, one corner carved away. ''But there can be. If you are able to create that sort of work on a consistent basis, Mrs. Montgomery, you could be one of the nation's best-known artists in miniature.''

Morganna reached blindly for the other stool. Sloan caught her arm and guided her to it.

''But—as you yourself pointed out—not everyone will be able to afford an original. To add to the problem, the time involved in each sculpture means that you can make only a relatively small number of figures, so even if you get a high price for each one, your income potential is limited. That's even more true if you want to maintain your artistic freedom and do only projects that inspire you.''

For a moment, she'd been walking on air—until reality deflated her once more. ''So I end up with another hobby,'' she said wryly. ''That's no surprise.''

His eyes, magnified by the thick lenses of his glasses, were intent on her. ''I can solve that problem. I want to buy the rights to reproduce your dolls. Your originals will

command premium prices from the few who can afford
them. But I can manufacture quality reproductions at a
reasonable price that miniature enthusiasts everywhere
will snap up by the thousands. And we'll both make—
oh, a lot of money.'' He took a business card from his
wallet and handed it to her. ''You think it over, Mrs.
Montgomery. And when you have some more dolls for
me to look at, give me a call.'' He bowed, a formal and
courtly gesture.

Morganna was still sitting at her worktable with the
business card in her hand, staring at the block of clay,
when Sloan came back from showing the man out. ''I
don't believe it,'' she whispered. ''I never dreamed of
anything like this. To have a mere hobby—a silly pastime—turn into something that would actually let me earn
enough money to—'' She had to stop and clear her
throat. ''To give me the freedom—''

''Amazing,'' Sloan said. He reached across her to pick
up a booklet which had been tucked behind the block of
clay.

The cool note in his voice startled her. ''Sloan? Aren't
you happy for me?''

''Of course I am. I'm thrilled. Where did you get this
catalog, Morganna?''

She had to pull herself back from a mist of happy
dreams even to think about it. ''Oh, is that the one from
Furnishings Unlimited? Surely you don't think I was
shopping? Jack Hamilton gave it to me. He'd thought
you'd like to see it.''

''I've seen it. Not this copy, of course.'' He folded the
catalog and put it in his back pocket. ''I'm going over to
the hospital to see Joel, and then I'll probably go to the
office for a while.''

''It's Sunday,'' she said blankly.

"I wouldn't want you to think I was lazing around the house expecting you to support me. Or getting in the way of artistic expression, either."

He was gone before Morganna had found her voice.

How perfectly ridiculous, she fumed. There was no understanding the masculine ego. Let a woman have just a smidgen of success and suddenly the man in her life was a quivering mass of wounded pride!

Of course, it wasn't as if Sloan didn't have reason for wounded pride right now. Perhaps it hadn't been terribly sensitive of her to crow over her sudden success, when his career was literally in ashes at the moment. Or to tell him how much she looked forward to freedom…

Creative freedom, she had meant. Surely he hadn't misunderstood that. After last night, he couldn't possibly have thought she meant that she wanted to be free of him. Had he?

She couldn't remember exactly what she'd said, but she seemed to recall mentioning money as well as freedom, in almost the same breath. There was a sick feeling in the pit of her stomach. Though it wasn't what she'd said or meant, there was no question in her mind of what Sloan had heard—he'd thought she was announcing her desire to repay the money he'd put forth to settle her father's debts. To buy her freedom.

She seized her car keys and the first coat her hand fell on, and was out the door, less than five minutes behind Sloan.

She found him in the hospital corridor, leaning against the wall outside Joel's room. "What's wrong?" she asked breathlessly.

"With Joel? Nothing more than usual. There's a physical therapist working with him."

"Oh. Of course." She felt like a fool. "Sloan…" She

didn't know how to begin. "Can we go get a cup of coffee or something? I need to talk to you."

The door of Joel's room opened, and a man in a white lab coat came out, nodded to them, and walked briskly down the hall.

"Maybe later," Sloan said and pushed the door open.

Morganna looked past him and saw the fire investigator coming down the hall, carrying a large carton. She tried to smother a sigh. Of all the people they didn't need right now...

"Imagine this," the investigator said cheerfully. "I was planning to stop by to see you, just as soon as I talked to Joel. You've saved me a trip."

"Delighted, I'm sure," Morganna muttered.

Joel looked pale from the workout, and there was sweat on his brow. "What an honor," he muttered.

"You don't look eager for company," Morganna said. "Maybe later, after you've had a chance to get your breath back—"

The investigator set his carton down. "Oh, this won't take but a minute."

Sloan didn't seem to have heard her at all.

The investigator leaned on the bed rail. "Try to think back, Joel. You told me there was some playhouse furniture in the office, but you couldn't remember if it was there on the night of the fire."

Sloan said, "It wasn't meant to be played with. And it was there when I left the office that night."

"You didn't tell me about that furniture before, Mr. Montgomery."

"I didn't think about it," Sloan said coolly. "There are probably a lot of other things I forgot to tell you about, too."

Joel said suddenly, as if he hadn't been listening, "I

don't think so. The picture in my mind is hazy, and I couldn't swear to it. But I don't think it was there when I went in that night.''

"You," Morganna muttered, "have a mighty inconvenient memory. And how would you know whether it was or not, unless you walked clear across the room to the window and tripped over it?''

The investigator was looking at her, but he was clearly addressing Joel. "Would you say that furniture was something Mr. Montgomery was fond of?''

"He wouldn't have had it in his office otherwise," Joel said.

The investigator lifted the lid from the carton he'd carried in, pulled aside a paper wrapping, and lifted out a two-foot-tall, mirrored bureau. "Do you recognize this, Mr. Montgomery?''

Morganna was stunned. She watched in utter disbelief as Sloan reached across the bed, pulled open the top drawer, and took out a package of antacid tablets.

"It's mine, yes." His voice was not quite steady.

"But it's not even scorched," she objected. "And the heat, if not the blast, would have broken the mirror. How did it escape the fire?''

"That's a really good question," the investigator said. "We found it in a storage locker just a couple of blocks from the factory. We don't yet know how it got there. But the receipt the owner dug out for us says the unit was rented by a man named Montgomery.''

Joel said bitterly, "So that's the way the wind blows.''

The investigator pulled a paper from his pocket. "Here's a copy of the receipt.''

Sloan studied it and handed it back. "It's not my signature. It's not a bad approximation, but it's not my signature.''

The investigator folded the paper away. "Why would anybody hide these things and use your name?"

"Why would I use my own name? I'm not a moron. If I was going to hide these things there are a hundred better places."

"Like in your house, where your wife might see them? Not likely. Why didn't you call the police that night, Mr. Montgomery? You say that Joel here told you he'd seen men running from the building. You were carrying a cell phone. Why didn't you ask for help?"

"I didn't want to jump at shadows. I thought I'd go look the situation over first."

"All right. Why didn't you take your friend Mr. Hamilton with you? I understand he volunteered to go, but you told him to stay at the restaurant."

"I didn't see any need to break up the party completely."

"I see. And when the fire started, why didn't you call for help then? Surely you hadn't left the phone in your car."

"No, it was in my pocket."

Morganna couldn't take any more. "He was getting Joel out of the building. As long as you're jumping on details, what about the clothes? It was Sloan who told the nurses to be sure to keep Joel's clothes because you'd want them."

"You don't think they'd have noticed the gasoline smell without his help?" The investigator's eyes were wide with interest.

"He was being the hero," Joel said. "So what was it, Sloan? Insurance again?"

"Again?" The investigator's tone was crisp.

Joel raised a hand as if to gesture, and let it drop feebly against the blanket. "Oh, I don't mean he's done it before, exactly. But there was that business about Morganna's father's life insurance. The company didn't have to pay on a suicide, but Sloan found a clause in the fine print and threatened to take them to court.''

Morganna had stopped listening. Clearly someone had removed the furniture and stored it under Sloan's name, in order to frame him. But who would have done that? Who *could* have? And why? If she could just stay calm and think... But her brain was racing with the picture of Sloan being led away in handcuffs. Panic was closing in on her, tightening her muscles till she could scarcely breathe.

"It wasn't fraud, exactly, to make them pay," Joel was saying, "but..."

"You *weasel.*" Morganna's words seemed to burst forth. "Trying to throw suspicion on Sloan, after everything you owe him—"

"Everything I owe him?" Joel's voice had a vicious edge. "Including getting blown through a window and having my life destroyed, you mean?"

"It wasn't his fault. Why did you even go into the building that night? He told you not to. Why did you walk into the office? As soon as you got to the door, you'd have smelled the natural gas. Why didn't you just turn on the overhead light?"

"Maybe I did. I don't remember."

Sloan shook his head. "There were no regular lights on when I came in, just the security lamps. The first light I saw was the explosion."

Morganna scoffed, "You don't remember whether you flipped a switch, but you remember seeing the furniture? You'd have had to go clear around the desk to see it." She paused. "You could almost have touched the desk lamp from the door, but you didn't do that. You walked all the way around—that's what you must have done. That's why you got blown out the window. If you'd just leaned over the desk and touched the lamp, you'd have been blown back toward the door. Right?'' She turned to the investigator.

He looked thoughtful. ''It seems likely, yes.''

''So why did you go into the office at all?'' It was a hopeless question, of course. How could Joel answer when he didn't remember?

None of it makes any sense, she thought. *Nothing fits. Unless all the time we've been looking at it from the wrong side...*

She said slowly, ''We've been assuming the trap was intended for the following morning, when Sloan came to work. But it couldn't have been.''

The investigator raised an eyebrow. ''You seem very certain.''

''The natural gas,'' Morganna said impatiently. ''There would have been so much of it by morning that no one could have gotten all the way to Sloan's office without an air tank. They'd have smelled it first—they couldn't have missed that rotten-egg smell—and called for help.''

''If a chance spark hadn't set it off long before that,'' Sloan agreed.

''So there would have been no reason for the lightbulb, because nobody could have gotten far enough to set it off. That means the trap was intended to go off that night, when the factory was dark.''

Sloan said, ''I was supposed to walk into the office, smell the gas, turn on the light to check things out, and—''

Morganna shivered. The picture was all too real, the trap all too threatening. If Joel hadn't gone into the office,

Sloan would have. If Joel hadn't seen a man running from the building...

But the man he said he'd seen had proved he hadn't been anywhere near the factory that night. So the question became who Joel had seen.

If he had seen anyone at all. Because if he hadn't...

She stared at the man in the bed. He couldn't have been lying, she thought. Joel had been hurt by the booby trap, so he couldn't have been the one who set it. Unless...

"It went off by mistake," she whispered.

She turned to look at Sloan, and was startled to see that he did not look surprised. Obviously he had reached the same conclusion, even before she had made the connection. But how had he known?

As if he'd read her mind, Sloan said, "The catalog." He tugged it out of his pocket.

Pieces dropped into place in Morganna's mind. He was holding the Furnishings Unlimited catalog which he had picked up from her worktable less than an hour before. The one Jack Hamilton had given her, bearing the wrong address which had sent it all the way to the Omaha warehouse before it was delivered to him—the same wrong address that Jack had been teasing Sloan about at the restaurant the night of the fire.

But how could a firm in direct competition with Sticks & Stones have gotten that particular, exact wrong address? In only one way that she could see—it had come from Sticks & Stones' own records.

The records that had been more or less destroyed in the fire. Which meant the address had been passed along before the fire happened.

Things that aren't supposed to be there, the fire investigator said he always looked for. *And things that are supposed to be there, but aren't.*

Sloan said, almost gently, "What else did you sell, Joel, besides the customer list?"

"What the hell are you talking about?"

"Furnishings Unlimited had to get it somewhere. What did they promise you? Money? A job? That whole business of getting hold of their catalog early was a bluff, wasn't it? Such a good, loyal little corporate spy you were. Then you set the fire, not only to paralyze Sticks & Stones but to cover up the fact that you'd scrambled all our records, after you made copies for the competition—"

The fire investigator shifted from one foot to the other. "That's a mighty big accusation, Mr. Montgomery. You wouldn't happen to have any real evidence, I suppose?"

Morganna stared at Joel. Even the unburned side of his face was red now, with anger. She frowned. There was something about his face—blistered and twisted on one side, with the beginnings of angry scars, while the other side was almost untouched…

If he'd been standing by the desk, inserting a booby-trapped lightbulb into the lamp, and it accidentally went off, how could he have gotten burned on just one side of his face?

Were they being unjust to suspect him? No, her instinct said. This had to be the answer. There were just a few pieces still missing…

"He couldn't have turned his head," Morganna said under her breath. "He'd have to have been looking at the lamp while he worked. And when the bulb exploded, the gasoline would have hit him squarely across the face."

"But it didn't," the investigator said. "If it had, we'd

have suspected him immediately. But a glancing blow like the one he took—'' He shook his head. ''The bulb couldn't have gone off while he was working on it. He'd have been burned worse.''

''But then why did it blow up at all? Why didn't he just walk out and leave the trap for Sloan, as he'd intended to do?''

''If he'd brushed any metal part of the lamp,'' Sloan said, ''it would have turned the lamp on.''

''Did he know it was touch-controlled?'' the investigator asked.

''Yes,'' Sloan said. ''He did.''

''But that just means he'd have been extra-careful not to touch it,'' Morganna objected.

''He was in a hurry,'' Sloan pointed out. ''He was surprised when I told him where I was, and that I'd be at the factory in a matter of minutes.''

Morganna looked at the investigator. ''But you said it would take time to rig the lightbulb. Unless he'd done that beforehand. Of course—that's why there was no container for the gasoline; it was already in the bulb when he went into the factory that night. But why did it explode?''

Morganna closed her eyes. She wanted to hit her head against something in utter frustration. Why couldn't she think? Of course she was tired, they'd hardly slept at all last night. And she was stressed, but—

Suddenly she saw the lamps in Sloan's bedroom once more, glowing softly...

''Touch sensors get confused when the electricity goes off,'' she said suddenly. ''And the lamps turn on when it's restored.''

''Not good enough,'' the investigator said quietly.

"There wasn't a storm that night. The power didn't go out."

Morganna sighed. "And I suppose it would have been just too strange, anyway, to have a flicker at precisely the wrong moment.... Unless he unplugged the lamp." Triumph rang in her voice. "He knew it was controlled by touch, and he didn't want to take a chance of bumping it wrong while he was putting in the bulb. So he pulled the plug, put in the bulb, plugged the lamp back in, and it blew up. But he wasn't standing right by the lamp then. He was beside the wall outlet, probably leaning over—so he didn't take the full strength of the blast. It got him from the side instead. And since he was standing by the window—"

Joel was staring at her with hatred in his eyes. "Damn you, Morganna," he said. "And to think I felt so sorry for you, being stuck with a man you hated, that I tried to eliminate—" He stopped abruptly.

Morganna was stunned. "*That's* why you tried to kill Sloan? Because you thought I hated him?"

"No," Sloan said. "It's a noble excuse, trying to rescue the damsel in distress, but that wasn't the reason. He destroyed the business and scrambled the records—and tried to kill me—so in the confusion nobody would notice that there was money missing." His voice was almost gentle. "And you nearly got by with it, Joel, because even when I realized Sticks & Stones had been slowly and systematically robbed, I didn't think it could be you who was guilty. You don't live extravagantly, you don't play the horses, you don't even hang around with women who have expensive tastes. But you got greedy—and it was the pittance that Furnishings Unlimited paid you for the mailing list that finally gave you away." He tossed the catalog onto the bed. "Where's the money, Joel?

Parked in an offshore bank till you collected enough to make a run for it?''

The investigator said, ''Well, son? We'll find out... you might as well tell us. Let me get somebody in here to read you your rights, and then we can talk about the fire.''

''I'm not saying another word,'' Joel growled. ''Not without a lawyer.''

It's all right, Morganna thought. *Sloan is free.* She leaned against him, suddenly limp with relief. ''My darling—''

Joel gave a loud, humorless laugh. ''Isn't that touching,'' he drawled. ''Great job, Sloan. You married her to get even with her old man, and now she's panting for you.''

''Knock it off, Joel.'' Sloan's voice was low and cold.

''What are you talking about?'' Morganna asked.

''Guess you never told her why you married her, right, Sloan? Want me to?''

''Don't do something I'll make you regret, Joel.''

''What are you going to do,'' Joel jeered, ''haul me out of the hospital bed and sock me in the face when I can't even make a fist to defend myself? He didn't propose to you so he could be your white knight, princess, if that's what you're thinking. It wasn't because he felt sorry for you and your dear old mama. And it wasn't even that he had a hankering to join high society. Did he tell you what your father did to his father, all those years ago?''

She looked uncertainly at Sloan. *I don't want to believe him,* she thought. And yet there was a note of certainty in Joel's voice that forced her to keep listening.

''That's why he was keeping an eye on the Ashworths. Not because he was fascinated with you, but because he was waiting for his chance to get even with your father. That's why he engineered meeting you at that charity thing. And that's why he had me investigating the family. Then Burke died, and he was out of Sloan's reach. But you were still there.''

"Come on, Morganna," Sloan said. "We don't have to listen to this.''

She couldn't move; she stood frozen by the bedside.

Joel went on, his voice inexorable. "I was curious, you see. So I kept looking. I know all about the deal that went bad because Sloan's father didn't realize that Burke Ashworth's word wasn't worth the hot air that went into it. Did Sloan tell you that was what forced his father into bankruptcy? That's why Sloan had to drag himself up every rung of the ladder—and with every step, he remembered your father and what he had done to the Montgomerys.''

She was staring at Sloan. *Give me a reason not to believe him,* she begged.

"Sweetheart," Joel said almost gently, "whatever he told you, the truth is that he married you so he could take his revenge. And a *primo* kind of revenge he's made it, too.''

CHAPTER TEN

SLOAN'S face had gone pale. But it wasn't shock he was feeling, Morganna realized. It was fury. He hadn't been taken off guard, stunned by a whopper of a lie. He was enraged that Joel had dared to tell the truth.

I have wanted you for so long, Sloan had told her last night. Morganna had thought he meant the six months he had patiently waited for her to truly become his wife. But now the words took on another, more sinister meaning.

Exactly how long had he waited for his revenge? How many years?

Revenge... Nasty as the word was, Morganna thought, it was a pale description of what he had actually accomplished. Owning her—displaying her as the trophy wife she was—apparently hadn't been enough to satisfy him. Sloan had wanted even more. So he'd lulled her into falling in love with him, and only when he'd possessed not only her body but her soul had he been content.

He had boasted once that he didn't need to coerce her because she would come to him of her own free will. And she had. How that must have delighted him!

No wonder last night had seemed so special for him. It had represented his final triumph over the family that had destroyed his father.

She smiled up at him. "I don't think the inspector needs us here any longer, darling." She watched relief flood his eyes and felt ill. Without a glance at Joel, she put her hand on Sloan's arm and let him guide her out of the room.

171

In the hallway, he stopped and turned her toward him. "You didn't believe him."

He hadn't really asked a question, she realized, and his voice held an odd note of strain—as if he was trying to convince himself that she had dismissed Joel as nothing but a troublemaker. It might be interesting, if she only had the patience, to see whether Sloan would admit the truth eventually. But she had no time for games.

She pulled her hand away as if touching him had scorched her. "Oh, I believe him all right."

He reached for her. "Morganna—"

She ducked, and his hands closed on empty air instead of coming to rest on her shoulders. "I simply wasn't going to give Joel the satisfaction of making a scene for his enjoyment. And please don't insult me by saying you can explain—because there's no justifying this one, Sloan."

She was turning away when the investigator came out of Joel's room. "I want to thank you both. You handed me the last piece I needed."

"The last piece?" Morganna said in disbelief. "We handed you the whole thing!"

Sloan said, "I hope you don't expect us to believe that you were onto Joel all along."

"Not from the very beginning, no. If it makes you feel better, I never seriously thought it was you, Mr. Montgomery, because this fire didn't fit your personality."

"You could have fooled me." Sloan's voice was dry.

The investigator grinned, and then sobered. "I'm sorry about putting you through all this—both of you. I've been pretty sure for days that it was Joel, but I couldn't find the motive—you're right, Montgomery, he hasn't spent beyond his income and he doesn't appear to gamble. And I also couldn't explain exactly how that explosion could have gotten him by accident.'' He smiled at Morganna. ''Thanks for helping out there.''

''My pleasure,'' she said dryly.

''Besides, every bit of evidence I had was circumstantial, and it could all point at least two ways. Nothing about the way the fire started, or the way Joel was burned, ruled out the possibility that he was innocent. For instance, strolling across an office full of leaking natural gas is certainly stupid, but it isn't a crime. He could say he heard something from the factory floor and walked over to the window to check it out—and how could we prove he didn't? People do stupid things when they're under stress.''

''Why did he turn the gas on first?'' Sloan asked. ''It doesn't make sense.''

The investigator shrugged. ''The original plan was probably to install the trick lightbulb, then flip on the gas as he left. But it's possible that turning on the gas was an afterthought—maybe he had doubts at the last minute of how effective his gasoline bomb would be. By the way, we checked the ceiling light from your office and found that the bulbs were all loose. Again, there's no proving it—I suppose if the bulbs weren't put in tightly in the first place, the blast could have vibrated the fixture and loosened them. But I'm betting Joel unscrewed the bulbs just enough so the wall switch wouldn't work, so you'd have likely walked over to the desk and turned on the lamp.''

Morganna shivered.

''But if I'd gone into court with that kind of evidence,'' the investigator said, ''the attorneys would have blown all kinds of holes in it and Joel would have walked out a free man. Take the homeless guy who lives in the empty lot across the street. He saw Joel going in and out that night—but he didn't see him moving the furniture, and without that his testimony would be practically useless. We might have proved that the signature on the receipt from the storage unit was Joel's handwriting, but it was too small a sample to be definitive, and that's the sort of thing that expert witnesses can argue about for months at a time. The only way I could see to break Joel down was to make him feel so secure that he'd start to point fingers, and then he'd almost certainly incriminate himself. He was doing it beautifully, by the way—conveniently remembering things like the little furniture—even before you and Mrs. Montgomery started working out the puzzle.''

"Happy to be of service," Sloan said ironically.

The investigator grinned. "I'm sure—but thanks anyway. Well, I'll let you two go on about your business. As soon as we've filed charges, I'll notify the insurance people, and that should speed up the process considerably." The investigator went back into Joel's room.

The silence was thick. "Morganna—"

"I don't want to hear it, Sloan. I'm going home. I don't care what you do, or where you go." She zipped her coat and walked down the long hall. Without looking back, she knew that he watched her until she reached the first bend in the corridor. It was as much as she could do to hold her head high and not run, in her eagerness to get away from him to some quiet place where she could think.

The unseasonable snow had snarled traffic, and she was happy to finally reach the peaceful side streets of Pemberton Place. The neighbors next door were outside with their twins, building a snow family. The picture wrenched Morganna's heart.

That could be Sloan and me playing with our kids, in a few years, she thought. *If only Joel hadn't...*

She caught herself up short. Joel hadn't created this problem, he'd only exposed it. Surely she wasn't so foolish that she would rather it had remained hidden!

A secret like that couldn't have remained entirely concealed, anyway. Even if it had never exactly come into the open, the poison of Sloan's hidden motives would have seeped through every aspect of their marriage, ruining any hope of happiness. Refusing to face things didn't make them go away; it only made them more explosive in the long run.

She turned her back on the happy family, now engaged in a snowball fight, and went inside.

Abigail came hastily out of the drawing room. "Is it true, Morganna?"

For an instant, Morganna wasn't sure what she was asking about.

"Sloan called Selby, so he could pass the word to the staff. Was it really Joel who set the fire?"

Morganna nodded.

Abigail closed her eyes for an instant in what looked like a prayer of relief and thankfulness. "And I wasted all that effort feeling sorry for him," she mused. "Well, if that's under control, too...I think I'll go see if I can get a ticket on this afternoon's plane."

Morganna was taken aback. "Where are you going?"

"Home, of course. Now that you and Sloan have everything settled between you, you don't need me hanging around and getting in the way of what promises to be a delightful honeymoon."

A delightful honeymoon...yes, this morning it had looked like that. What a difference a few hours could make.

"And Robert's been getting impatient for me to come home, anyway."

"Who's Robert?" Morganna said it only because it seemed to be expected of her.

"The man I've been seeing. I told you about him."

"The one you said was stalking you? Mother—"

"Did I imply that?" Abigail sounded faintly surprised. "I thought I said he was pursuing me, which he's certainly been doing."

"You told me you came to Lakemont to avoid him!"

"Well, yes, I did say that. It made a very handy excuse for coming up to check on you, and it wasn't quite a lie, because I thought it was time to see how much we'd really miss each other."

"And did you?" Morganna asked feebly.

"Of course, dear. Who do you think I've been talking to, all the hours I've been on the phone? Anyway, I'm so glad that everything is going to work out just fine for you and Sloan." She smiled. "If he's not coming straight home, I'll use the phone in his library to get my ticket and tell Robert when to pick me up."

Morganna nodded. "Go ahead."

She knew she should correct her mother's mistaken impression. But her own wounds were too fresh; she couldn't possibly explain to Abigail what she hadn't come to terms with yet herself. She needed a little time to sort out what she would say; there was nothing to be gained for any of them by telling Abigail that Sloan had set out to take his revenge—and succeeded.

Soon Abigail would be back in Phoenix, and presumably occupied with…what was his name? Robert, that was it. So Morganna would have a little space to figure out how much to tell her mother and how to explain the way they sorted out the mess. Whatever it was they decided to do.

She frowned. What was she thinking of? It would be a divorce, of course. What other option was there?

Unless Sloan utterly refused to let her go—but that was impossible. He could no longer count on her sense of loyalty and fairness forcing her to keep her end of the deal, when he had betrayed her. She didn't owe him anything more.

Black misery descended on her. How perfectly ironic, she thought, that the thing she had longed for only a couple of weeks ago—freedom from Sloan—now looked so bleak.

Once she had looked at the six-month history of their marriage and dreaded the thought of spending six years as Sloan's wife. Last night, if she had been capable of thinking at all, she might have looked forward with pleasure to the hope of six decades with him beside her.

In fact, she'd had just six hours of happiness. Six hours of dreaming that they might make a future and a family together. Six hours of thinking that she was important to him.

Oh, she was important to Sloan Montgomery, all right, she thought grimly. It was just in a very different way than she had hoped for.

Dusk had settled, the temperature was dropping, and the snow that had melted into the streets all day had frozen once more and formed icy spots. Morganna dropped her mother off at the airport terminal, and by the time she had carefully negotiated the drive all the way back across Lakemont, Abigail's plane was halfway to Phoenix.

Relieved to be back in Pemberton Place, Morganna parked her car in the garage beside the black Jaguar and went inside. The door of Sloan's library was closed, and the house was quiet except for the click of flatware in the dining room, where Selby was setting the table for dinner.

The dining table looked very big, with only two places set, and the idea of sitting there and making polite conversation with Sloan was more than she could bear. "I'm not hungry tonight, Selby," she said. "I'm going to skip dinner and work instead. I don't want to be disturbed."

His hands stilled, but Selby was too self-disciplined to betray shock. "Very well, Miss Morganna."

In her miniature room, she dug a knife deep into the block of clay, tearing off a corner. Rhythmically she kneaded the clay into malleability and began shaping the torso of a grandmotherly woman.

She didn't know how much time had passed when the door quietly opened. She didn't look up. "I thought I made it clear that I didn't want to be disturbed."

"I know," Sloan said. "Selby told me."

Her fingers clenched convulsively, turning the half-finished figure into a lump of clay indistinguishable from the rest of the block.

So here we are, she thought. *This is the room where it all started—and this is where it will end.*

Sloan pulled out the other stool from her worktable and sat down. "Is that how you plan to handle this?" He sounded almost casual. "Separate lives under the same roof, just the way it used to be?"

"Not quite the way it used to be," Morganna said deliberately. "I had some respect for you, then."

She heard his quick intake of breath and braced herself. But he didn't answer. Instead, a full minute passed before he said, "I'm glad about the figurines, Morganna.

They're good, and you deserve to be recognized for your art.''

"It remains to be seen how successful I'll be," she said quietly. "But if I can, I'll make sure you get back all the money you've paid out to settle my father's debts."

His voice was taut. "Do you think that's what I want?"

"Oh, no. I'm sure you'd rather have left things just the way they were last night. Much more comfortable for you."

"Dammit, Morganna—"

"Isn't that what you wanted? For me to pay the price for what he did? Fine, I'll pay—but this time I'm going to set the terms."

He slid off the stool and strode away. For a moment she thought he was leaving, but he paced across the room and back to stand beside her. "I know you said you didn't want to hear this. But you're going to listen, Morganna."

"I don't know why you'd think I owe you that much courtesy."

Refusing to face things doesn't make them go away. She'd told herself that just a few hours earlier. In this case, of course, dragging it all out wouldn't make it go away, either—but he was right about one thing. She needed to know exactly what had happened. Exactly why they had never stood a chance.

She shrugged and started to cut the block of clay into manageable clumps. "So if it will satisfy you, talk. Just don't expect me to believe everything you say. You told me you didn't even know my father—remember?"

"I said I'd never met him, and that was true."

"True, maybe, but misleading. Which you intended,

of course.'' She worked a lump of clay loose from the knife.

Sloan was silent for a moment, as if he was gathering his thoughts. "The details don't matter, I suppose. My father had a terrific idea for a business. At least he thought it was a terrific idea, and perhaps it was. Nobody ever had a chance to find out. At a businessmen's club, he ran into a sympathetic listener named Burke Ashworth, who was soon just as sold on the idea as my father was. He was so enthusiastic, in fact, that he agreed to back the business financially. They shook hands on the deal, and my father, in utter delight at getting his chance, rented a location and set up an office and bought raw materials and hired a crew. He did it with no cash, just his own signature, backed up by Burke Ashworth's promise.''

She knew what was coming, but knowing didn't make it any less painful to hear.

"Then he went back to your father and gave him the list of expenses and asked for the money. Burke Ashworth denied ever making any such agreement.''

"He implied that your father had heard what he wanted to hear?''

"Worse than that,'' Sloan said. "He said straight out—in public—that he'd refused his support, so my father had deliberately set out to defraud all those people by using his name. There was no recourse—people still believed Burke Ashworth back then. They didn't have any reason to believe my father. He ended up declaring bankruptcy because he didn't have any choice, but he was still paying off those debts the day he died. He was a bitter, resentful, beaten man, made old long before his time by a lying cheat named Ashworth.''

Morganna said, "So you honored your father's memory by holding a grudge and becoming just as bitter and resentful as he was. Congratulations.''

"I didn't have time to do any such thing. I kept an eye out for your father, yes, and I hoped that someday he'd get his comeuppance and I'd be there to see it. But I was too busy scraping together enough money to get an education, and later to get my business going, to worry about revenge.''

"But once Sticks & Stones had made you a million-aire, you had time on your hands,'' Morganna mused. "Oh, and maybe I should ask—where do I come into this?''

"You came into it just about a year ago,'' Sloan said. "I offered to donate furniture for the women's shelter, and I got roped into being an adviser to the board of directors. So there I was, not quite knowing what I was doing, and suddenly you appeared—part of the fund-raising committee.''

"And they say charity work is good for you,'' Morganna muttered.

"So I scraped a meeting, just to see what you were like.''

"Too bad I didn't disappoint you.''

"No, it was apparent from the beginning that you had just as much charm as your father did.''

Morganna gritted her teeth. It had obviously not been a compliment. "So you waited for your chance. And my father, selfish jerk that he was, handed you the weapon you needed.''

"I know how it looks, Morganna.'' Sloan sounded tired. "But I didn't marry you to get even with your father.''

She was incredulous. "You expect me to believe that now?''

"No. I don't know. Hell, at the time, *I* thought it was revenge I had in mind. It made such a neat little package—using you to regain everything your father cost mine. But that wasn't why I did it. I didn't fully understand what I was doing until last night."

"If you have the unbelievable gall to tell me that going to bed with me was some kind of revelation—"

He shook his head. "No. It was before that. At the Carousel Ball, you stood by me, when you didn't have to. I took advantage of your misfortune—but when you had the chance to pay me back, you didn't do it. Loyalty was something your father never understood. But you're true to the core, Morganna."

She was frightened that he would pursue that thought and start wondering if there was some special reason why she felt loyal to him. "Just another way to display my charm," she said coolly.

"No, it reminded me of the first time I ever saw you, at that charity fund-raiser. One of the little kids from the shelter had taken a tumble and was crying, and you picked him up."

She didn't remember. "So? You expected I'd kick him out of my way?"

"He wiped his runny nose on the shoulder of your designer dress. And you didn't get angry, or scold him, or even set him down. You laughed and hugged him closer."

Morganna shrugged. "I doubt anyone will nominate me for a Nobel prize on the strength of that."

"I couldn't see it at the time," he said meditatively. "But as I look back, it was obvious. That was the moment I fell in love with you."

Morganna dropped her knife. It bounced off the worktable and clattered against the hardwood floor, but she didn't hear it.

I fell in love with you....

"But I simply couldn't admit to myself that I'd taken a dive for Burke Ashworth's daughter, because of what it might lead to. Was I going to sit down with the man for dinner? Buy him a tie for Father's Day? Not a chance. So I didn't let myself think about any of that. I just watched you, and waited. When he died, and I found out what a spot he'd left you and Abigail in—"

"You decided to be a hero." She was having trouble breathing.

His mouth twisted. "No. I decided to be a villain. I didn't exactly intend to punish you, or deliberately make your life miserable. What I planned to do was show you what it was like to be on the receiving end of that kind of selfishness."

"You think I didn't already know? One thing you have to say about my father, at least in the last few years. He wasn't two-faced. He was a self-centered jerk in everything he did." Morganna shook her head. "Whereas you...I suppose you're going to tell me that you brought home diamond bracelets to show me how selfish you were?"

"In a way I did," he said levelly, "because I knew you hated wearing those things. You couldn't wait to get rid of the jewelry, could you? And of me. So where do we go from here, Morganna?"

She couldn't answer. He had said he loved her—and yet if she told him now that she wanted to be free, it seemed he would let her go without a qualm and without an instant's hesitation. But surely, if he cared for her as he'd said he did... She shook her head in confusion.

He seemed to take the gesture as an answer. "I'll do

my best to make it neat and tidy. The house is yours, and the car, and as far as living expenses—''

It was tearing her up to listen to him. ''Stop it, Sloan.''

''Whatever you want, Morganna. I did it all backwards, and I don't have any right to ask for a break now. So if you want me to leave—''

She said softly, ''What if I don't?''

He looked at her for a long moment in silence, and then he rubbed his temples as if his head hurt. His words came slowly and unsteadily. ''It was driving me crazy to live with you and yet not have you as my wife—and that was before I even understood how I felt. Morganna, I don't think I can go back to the way it was.''

''I'm not asking you to. Do you know why I came to the hospital after you this morning?''

''No,'' he admitted. ''I was too focused on Joel right then to wonder why you were there.''

''You were cold, almost angry, when you left. I thought it was because of the figurines—''

He shook his head. ''I'd just spotted that catalog and realized what Joel had done. But I didn't know how to prove it, and that was chewing me up inside. It wasn't anything you said.''

''I thought you believed that I wanted to be able to pay you back and be free of you. So I came running after you to tell you...'' She swallowed hard. ''To tell you I don't want to be free.''

He sounded as if he'd been kicked in the solar plexus. ''Morganna—''

''I tried to hate you,'' she said. ''But all I could hate was the idea that I didn't matter to you, that I was only a display rack for clothes and jewelry. A trophy to show how important and successful and generous you were. You told me that was all you required, Sloan, and I agreed to the bargain. But then I started to want more. To need more. And I detested myself for falling in love with a man who saw me as nothing more than an inter-changeable convenience—''

"No," he said breathlessly. "Never that. It's you I need, Morganna. Only you. Always you."

Then she was in his arms, and she was laughing and crying at the same time, exhilarated at being close to him but still suffering the lingering terror of how nearly it had all gone wrong.

He held her till she calmed, and then he laid his cheek against her hair. "I wanted to tell you last night that I loved you. But I was afraid it would frighten you—that you'd be scared of what I expected, or wanted. And I thought, since we'd reached a kind of truce, that there was time for me to win you over slowly. So I just held you, and hoped that your heart would hear what mine was saying."

"I did hear. At least, until Joel had to go mess things up."

"You know," Sloan said thoughtfully, "I'm almost glad he did. Because, if he hadn't blown the whistle, I could never have confessed it. I couldn't just say, 'Gee, honey, there's a little something you should know about why I married you.' Telling you would have hurt you for no good purpose. But how could I have kept it secret? It would have contaminated everything between us."

It was exactly what she had thought herself. Nevertheless... "I'm still not sending him a thank-you note."

"I doubt he'll be watching the mail for one." Sloan sobered. "I've got a lot of rebuilding to do, honey. It's going to be a slow process, getting Sticks & Stones up and running again. Getting my customers back."

"If you're telling me that finances are going to be tight, I'll get busy making figurines."

He shook his head. "You'll get busy making figurines because you want to, not because we need the money. The San Francisco deal came through after all, and they're willing to wait till we're back in operation. It'll be the first big job we do. Anyway, as far as finances go, you've already done your part by giving up your jewelry."

"Sloan…" Her voice was small.

"Yes, darling?"

"I would like to have my wedding ring back, if it isn't already gone."

He reached into his pocket. "I picked it up before I came in here, hoping it would bring me luck—so now that it's done me all the good it possibly can, it needs to go back where it belongs."

She held out her hand, and he slid the slender, delicate platinum wedding band into place and kissed her hand, and then her mouth.

"How about this one?" he said, holding up her engagement ring. "I don't think I ever told you that I chose it because it was almost as bright as your eyes."

She blinked away tears. "You know perfectly well you never said anything so sentimental."

"Well, I thought it," he said unrepentantly. "The jewelry was never intended to buy you, Morganna. I just liked to see you wear it, because it helped to say you were mine."

"I know that now," she whispered.

"But now that I've really won the prize, I don't need to show you off as a trophy. So as far as the jewelry goes—"

"You've still got it all?"

He nodded. "Is there anything out of that pile that you'd like to have back?"

"Whatever you want to give me—as long as you give it with love this time."

"That's the same way I gave it last time," he said softly. "I just wasn't smart enough to know it then—or to tell you." He kissed her slowly and deeply. "But you can expect to hear a lot about it in the future."

Morganna relaxed against him, nestling close. "In that case," she said contentedly, "you can start telling me right now."

TO HAVE AND TO HOLD

Marriages meant to last!

They've already said "I do," but what happens
when their promise to love, honor and cherish
is put to the test?

Emotions run high as husbands and wives
discover how precious—and fragile—
their wedding vows are....
Will true love keep them together—forever?

Look out in Harlequin Romance® for:

HUSBAND FOR A YEAR
Rebecca Winters (August, #3665)

THE MARRIAGE TEST
Barbara McMahon (September, #3669)

HIS TROPHY WIFE
Leigh Michaels (October, #3672)

THE WEDDING DEAL
Janelle Denison (November, #3678)

PART-TIME MARRIAGE
Jessica Steele (December, #3680)

Available wherever Harlequin books are sold.

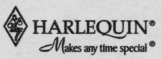

HARLEQUIN®
Makes any time special®

Visit us at www.eHarlequin.com   HRTHATHR

Harlequin invites you to walk down the aisle...

To honor our year long celebration of weddings, we are offering an exciting opportunity for you to own the Harlequin Bride Doll. Handcrafted in fine bisque porcelain, the wedding doll is dressed for her wedding day in a cream satin gown accented by lace trim. She carries an exquisite traditional bridal bouquet and wears a cathedral-length dotted Swiss veil. Embroidered flowers cascade down her lace overskirt to the scalloped hemline; underneath all is a multi-layered crinoline.

Join us in our celebration of weddings by sending away for your own Harlequin Bride Doll. This doll regularly retails for $74.95 U.S./approx. $108.68 CDN. One doll per household. Offer good while quantities of gifts last. Please allow 6-8 weeks for delivery. Offer good in the U.S. and Canada only. Become part of this exciting offer!

Simply complete the order form and mail to:
"A Walk Down the Aisle"

IN U.S.A	IN CANADA
P.O. Box 9057	P.O. Box 622
3010 Walden Ave.	Fort Erie, Ontario
Buffalo, NY 14269-9057	L2A 5X3

Enclosed are eight (8) proofs of purchase found in the last pages of every specially marked Harlequin series book and $3.75 check or money order (for postage and handling). Please send my Harlequin Bride Doll to:

_____
Name (PLEASE PRINT)

_____
Address   Apt. #

_____
City   State/Prov.   Zip/Postal Code

_____
Account # (if applicable)   **097 KIK DAEW**

HARLEQUIN®
Makes any time special ®

Visit us at www.eHarlequin.com

A Walk Down the Aisle
Free Bride Doll Offer
One Proof-of-Purchase

PHWDAPOPR2

If you enjoyed what you just read,
then we've got an offer you can't resist!

Take 2 bestselling
love stories FREE!
Plus get a FREE surprise gift!

Clip this page and mail it to Harlequin Reader Service®

IN U.S.A.	IN CANADA
3010 Walden Ave.	P.O. Box 609
P.O. Box 1867	Fort Erie, Ontario
Buffalo, N.Y. 14240-1867	L2A 5X3

YES! Please send me 2 free Harlequin Romance® novels and my free surprise gift. After receiving them, if I don't wish to receive anymore, I can return the shipping statement marked cancel. If I don't cancel, I will receive 6 brand-new novels every month, before they're available in stores! In the U.S.A., bill me at the bargain price of $3.15 plus 25¢ shipping & handling per book and applicable sales tax, if any*. In Canada, bill me at the bargain price of $3.59 plus 25¢ shipping & handling per book and applicable taxes**. That's the complete price and a savings of 10% off the cover prices—what a great deal! I understand that accepting the 2 free books and gift places me under no obligation ever to buy any books. I can always return a shipment and cancel at any time. Even if I never buy another book from Harlequin, the 2 free books and gift are mine to keep forever.

186 HEN DC7K
386 HEN DC7L

Name	(PLEASE PRINT)	
Address	Apt.#	
City	State/Prov.	Zip/Postal Code

* Terms and prices subject to change without notice. Sales tax applicable in N.Y.
** Canadian residents will be charged applicable provincial taxes and GST.
  All orders subject to approval. Offer limited to one per household and not valid to
  current Harlequin Romance® subscribers.
® are registered trademarks of Harlequin Enterprises Limited.

HROM01   ©2001 Harlequin Enterprises Limited